To A

JACOB:
THE WRESTLER

Thank you. May you
be blessed in reading
this story.

JACOB:

THE WRESTLER

A Novel

L I Z   C H U A

JACOB: THE WRESTLER
Copyright © 2023 Liz Chua

This is a work of fiction. While trying to remain faithful to the Biblical narrative surrounding Jacob's life, some characters, circumstances and conversations are works of imagination

Scripture quotations are from the New International Version (Zondervan) and the Complete Jewish translations of the Bible. Permissions below:

Scriptures taken from the Holy Bible, New International Version®, NIV®. Copyright © 1973, 1978, 1984, 2011 by Biblica, Inc.™ Used by permission of Zondervan. All rights reserved worldwide. www.zondervan.com The "NIV" and "New International Version" are trademarks registered in the United States Patent and Trademark Office by Biblica, Inc.™

Scriptures taken from the Complete Jewish Bible by David H. Stern. Copyright © 1998. All rights reserved. Used by permission of Messianic Jewish Publishers, 6120 Day Long Lane, Clarksville, MD 21029. www.messianicjewish.net.

Editors: Ruby Knudtson, Carolyn Matiisen
Cover Design: Joyce Chua
Book Layout: Angela Wagler

ISBN: 9798868041976
Imprint: Independently published

Liz Chua is less an historian of ancient events and more an eyewitness to them: her recreation of the story of Jacob has the weight and texture of lived experience, as though she's observed the scheming Patriarch's tumultuous life close up, from an unsafe distance. The effect is a tale that implicates us, embroils us, pulls us into itself like a man who ambushes us to wrestle us, and wound us, and bless us.

Mark Buchanan, Author of the David Trilogy

Liz Chua's novel, "Jacob: The Wrestler," creatively tells the story of Jacob and his family. The strength of her work is her sympathetic reflection on what each of these individuals would have felt in their struggles and hardships. Liz's insightful understanding of this family of dysfunction shows the timelessness of these narratives. The sorrows and passions of the ancient matriarchs and patriarchs are the same as those experienced in families today.

Rick Love, Pastor of Intercultural Ministries, Foothills Alliance Church

Remaining as true to the Biblical narrative as possible, Liz Chua takes you on the roller coaster ride of Jacob's life journey. In surprising twists and turns of dialogue and interaction, the chapters make the reader eager to know what's coming next. How Jacob gets to untangle himself from the tangles he unwittingly got himself in. Delving further we can often identify with his struggles. The transforming power of God leads Jacob to be renamed Israel, meaning the "man who wrestled with God".

Ruby Knudtson

I was given a copy of Liz Chua's book, "Jacob: The Wrestler" to read 'if I had time'. However, once I started to read, I couldn't put it down! It is not the rather dry biblical account of Jacob's nomadic life, but an exciting, gripping story of a man you get to know and empathize with. Liz's use of suspense and surprise kept me reading. She takes the bare facts and weaves them into a fascinating narrative. There is never a dull moment in this book!

Carolyn Matiisen

This story drew me in like I was an observer watching from the sideline—it allowed me to enter in and wonder what in the world was going to happen (even though I know the story)—it came alive and I felt like I was right there beside the characters listening in to their thoughts. Liz highlighted a kind of history and personality characteristics that I might have ignored and that I had not ever considered and now it is making me more curious and wonder—what is behind all of this—it leaves me asking questions, excited to read more.

Fern E.M. Buszowski, Author of "Embrace Life, Embrace Hope: Cultivating Wholeness and Resilience through the Unexpected"

*I dedicate this book to
my husband, Chris Chua,
whose enduring faith in God
pointed me to Jesus
and saved my soul.*

FOREWORD

If we could inhabit the ancient Middle Eastern world of the Biblical Patriarch, Jacob, what would it be like to follow in his footsteps? In this her first novel, Liz Chua skillfully draws you in as you explore the culture, the customs, the circumstances of that era, and particularly the emotions of the characters.

Remaining as true to the Biblical narrative as possible, Liz takes you on the roller coaster ride of Jacob's life journey. In surprising twists and turns of dialogue and interaction, the chapters make the reader eager to know what's coming next. How Jacob gets to untangle himself from the tangles he unwittingly finds himself in. Delving further we can often identify with his struggles. The transforming power of God leads Jacob to be renamed Israel, meaning the "man who wrestled with God".

Readers get to join the characters who influence and impact Jacob and see how their stories interweave with his, bringing truth to the saying that *'No Man is An Island'*. And behind it all, God has His eyes on the growth and development of each and every person. Through the years, we see how God uses unexpected circumstances and people to accomplish His purposes. And we ask ourselves, could that be true of our lives too?

Ruby Knudtson

AUTHOR'S NOTE

What seems like eons ago, the urge to write bubbled from deep within my being. Exactly when it began, I do not know. But like an underground spring making its way to the surface, it would meander and gurgle, meander and gurgle till I eventually put the thoughts down in print. Then like the release of a valve waiting to spout, the relief would come. In the words of a favorite author, "it is write or die".

And so one fine day I told the One behind that urge, "Lord, since you have seen fit to give me the joy of writing, I want to write your stories." It began with daily personal journaling, then to fulfilling a promise to my century-old mother to write her life-story, progressed to blogging about anything and everything that the One put into my heart or whispered into my ears, and finally to this first venture of a novel—a historical narrative.

Of all the characters in the Bible, the third Old Testament patriarch, Jacob, has always fascinated me. I find him so relatable, so human. Born the younger of twins, the less boisterous of the two, he always had to struggle to be heard, to be seen for who he was. Then, there was his latent desire for the spiritual, for a personal relationship with God, the God of his fathers. Born the eleventh of twelve children, many of whom are strong characters, in my growing up days I had quietly struggled to speak up. Then, there was always the knowledge that there was more to life than merely existing, and that there was a God. But amidst the plethora of gods surrounding my childhood and youth, who was the true and living God became my secret quest. So when I read about Jacob and then studied a bit more about his up and down life—wrestling with his sibling, wrestling for his father's attention, wrestling with himself, wrestling with his father-in-law, wrestling with God—it really hit a chord with me. I had to put my own wrestling to bed.

This book began in 2020 during the throes of the Covid 19 stay-at-home confinement. The perfect time for reflection and introspection. Day by day, the words came and my fingers typed fast trying to keep pace. Before the year's end, it was done. Then it sat untouched but continually percolating in the brain. For three years. My husband and a dear kindred friend would not let me forget it, though, till it went to print. That said, it is still a work of fiction. While trying to remain faithful to the Biblical narrative surrounding Jacob's life—ancestry, cultural background, era, etc.—several other characters are works of imagination, of what could have been.

I hope that in reading this novel, you will be able to resonate with one or more of the many characters and circumstances that God used to shape the life of Jacob. And in so doing, some of your own wrestlings will come to rest in the One who loves you with unfathomable love.

"I love to tell the story of unseen things above ... it satisfies my longing as nothing else can do."

TERAH FAMILY

Terah (father)
Abram/Abraham (son)
Sarai/Sarah (daughter-in-law)
Nahor (son)
Haran (son)

Milkah (granddaughter)
Lot (grandson)
Bethuel (grandson)
Rebekah (great-granddaughter)
Laban (great-grandson)
Leah (great-great-granddaughter)
Rachel (great-great-granddaughter)

ABRAHAM FAMILY

Sarah (wife) --------- **ABRAHAM** -------- Hagar (maid/concubine)
Isaac (son with Sarah)   Ishmael (son with Hagar)
Rebekah (daughter-in-law/grandniece)
Esau (grandson)
Jacob (grandson)

ISAAC FAMILY

Rebekah (wife) -------------------------------------- **ISAAC**
Esau (eldest twin son)
Jacob (youngest twin son)

JACOB FAMILY

Leah (1st wife) ------------ **JACOB** ------------ **Rachel** (2nd wife)
Reuben   Joseph
Simeon   Benjamin
Levi
Judah
Issachar
Zebulun
Dinah

Zilpah   **Bilhah**
(Leah's maid/Jacob's concubine)   (Rachel's maid/Jacob's concubine)
Gad   Dan
Asher   Naphtali

JACOB: THE WRESTLER

"They are all three, each one of his own account,
plotting this and plotting that."
(*Charles Spurgeon*)

One

ABRAHAM

Terah's grief was a torrent. A deluge of sorrow so heavy it threatened to send him over the other world with his son, Haran. Haran's sickness had begun with a pounding headache that worsened by the day. Weeks of oil extracts, poultices, and the finest of herbal teas failed to alleviate the affliction. The end came swiftly but all too cruelly. The ancients said sickness and death were the wages of sin. Fearing the curse of the gods upon his household, Terah led his bereaved family away from Ur's doom. As far away from the starless nights of death as he possibly could.

Abraham did not blame his father's despondency. Family was thick in their culture. To lose one's own, a healthy beloved man of a son at that, was to have a piece of one's heart savagely sliced out. Together with Sarah, Abraham helped Terah pack all their belongings onto the herds and headed out with brother Nahor, and Haran's family—son, Lot, and daughter, Milkah. The cavalcade set out westward and north.

With each long camel stride into the Mesopotamian desert somber silence intermingled with hope, anticipation and even hidden excitement. Impossible long arduous days under the unforgiving sun were relieved only by nights in the desert's bold beauty. Scattered rocks and boulders studded the arid ground. At times blinding blizzards of sand so fine stung their eyes through their thick head coverings. They sought refuge in the nooks and crannies of caves and valleys along the way. By day, they went forth in their sun-led trek, finding water in welcome oases. Always when needed. The marvel of it all never failed to escape Abraham. At the end of each day's sojourn, they rested their weary backs wrapping their goat-skin cloaks about them in the nighttime cold. Star-studded skies etched luminesce in Abraham's mind each time he beheld the heavenly display. Galaxies, stars and comets bespeckled the midnight sky. Exquisite beauty. Abraham sighed, wondrous delight flooding his soul. The cacophonous silence, a holy reverence. It evoked a mysterious deep-seated desire to commune with the Creator of such wondrous sights. But for the hard looks from their father's eyes, Abraham would have set up an altar there and then to the God he had not yet known. Wordlessly Abraham prayed for creation's soothing balm to be upon Terah.

Their journey north of the 'land between the rivers' entailed many stops for the family. At Haran one such break was made for the wedding between Nahor and niece, Milkah. Milkah was of age. And Nahor had been alone long enough. It was custom. No one questioned the marriage. The union mended Terah's broken heart. It did the old man good to know that his grandchildren would no longer be left fatherless. Perhaps it was fated that it was at Haran that Terah took his last breath on earth. At 205 years, the aged one was content that his journey ended where his sons' families would begin theirs.

One tranquil winter night after the mourning period for the deceased was past, Abraham wandered alone into the dark. A rare moonless night. Terah, their patriarch was gone. The mantle of family responsibility now lay on his shoulders. Abraham missed his father's presence, holding dear their many man-to-man conversations as they journeyed high on camel backs. Now away from the family camp, Abraham had taken to speaking to the One who had led them thus far. Unlike his father, Abraham somehow believed there could only be one Creator of the wondrous universe. And on this sojourn he had found himself speaking to that Being. In his mind mostly and in whispers sometimes. And when he was a safe distance from the rest as with this night, he spoke aloud his thoughts. "Great One, I know you are there. I sense your presence everywhere. Will you speak a word to me tonight? My *abba* is no more. It is just my brother and I and both our families. I know not how to lead as our father did."

To his astonishment Abraham heard these words, *"Get yourself out of your country, away from your kinsmen and away from your father's house, and go to the land that I will show you."*

Turning around to see if anyone was about and heard what he thought he had heard, Abraham chided himself that he had walked out alone. Who was there to verify the mysterious voice? Those mystifying words? Then barely out of his reverie, the voice spoke again.

"I will make you a great nation, I will bless you, and I will make your name great; and you are to be a blessing. I will bless those who bless you, but I will curse anyone who curses you; and by you all the families of the earth will be blessed."

The swirl of words was heady. Abraham had no time to ponder or wonder. His spontaneous response stunned even himself. "What are you saying, Great One. I have only known a tent as home since we left Ur. We have been mere nomads moving from place to place."

Split-second later strange words spilled from his mouth unrestrained. "But—but since you say, 'Go!' I will...go. Since you say you will show me the land of your leading, I will follow your direction. Only let my family not think me insane. Only let them be willing as I am willing to believe what I hear. This is preposterous! But your Spirit grips me so."

Calmly Abraham returned to the camp, crawled beneath the covers into his wife's warmth and slept. More peaceful than he had ever known.

A new dawn arose. Nothing had changed. Yet everything was different now for Abraham. Was it only a mere six hours ago that he had laid his head upon the pillow? Was it a dream that he had heard the transcendent voice? Said that he would heed the strange words? Baffling in its clarity. Resolute in its promises. Yet since their first setting out from Ur he had never felt such peace. At once he decided to test the waters before doubt and fear set in as it certainly would.

"Sarah, Nahor, I have something important to share with

you. Spare me a moment before you head into the day. You too, nephew." Abraham gestured for Lot to join them.

"What is it, brother? I have much business to attend to this morning. Can it not wait till noon?" Nahor responded not with a little irritation.

Abraham stayed his ground, saying, "No, it cannot wait, brother. It involves all of you. Please, sit. Listen. I will not detain you more than necessary. But it would do my heart good that you hear me out."

Sensing the seriousness in Abraham's tone, the family left their morning chores and gathered around him. Even Milkah edged her pregnant body beside her husband. Uncle Abraham was now head of the family. What he had to say would be of consequence hereon.

"You know I am but a simple man. Plain in speech as in manner. Therefore I will not mince words." This made everyone lean in a little closer, sit up straighter, ears keen, senses fully attuned.

"Last night, while you were all asleep, I went for a walk. A windless night as ever there was one. A night when sounds around are magnified a thousandfold. And, no, Lot, I am not referring to your rumbling snores." Abraham smiled at his nephew as he began the telling of his unique encounter with *Yahweh*. The unmentionable Name somehow just slipped out from his lips as surreptitiously as it had just entered his mind while he was speaking. Taken aback by this sudden revelation, Abraham was emboldened in his continuation. Raptly the family listened, each one taking in the man's slow words as it was being shared. They had never before heard

Abraham speak with such clarity of purpose, such assuredness of confidence, such humility of spirit. The absolute power of his words was as God's breath. Otherworldly. Mesmerizing.

Abraham had barely finished his last word when Lot declared for all to hear, "I will go with you, Uncle!"

"So will I, husband," added Sarah just as surely.

Abraham took their responses to be the affirmation that he had asked for of *Yahweh*. Turning then to Nahor seated across from him, he waited as the two brothers locked eyes. Abraham was not surprised when with tears rolling slowly down his rugged bearded face, Nahor explained, "Brother, I envy your encounter with the Almighty. Your face shines with inexplicable joy and peace. You are a privileged man to be able to hear from the Unknown One himself. My family and I will not stand in your way. You must go as you believe you have been so instructed. May your faith in Him sustain you all. May His strong presence go with you away from our father's house and from all your kin to the land He will show you. Milkah and I will pray you will be blessed as you have been promised. We will stay here in Haran. This is where our father is buried. This is home for us. And we will be here when it is your time to return."

Oh, that every momentous decision could be so harmoniously agreeable. So quickly discernible as from the supernatural. Talk not about the absurdity of it all. That night after everyone had retired, Abraham went once more to the spot where he had heard from *Yahweh*. Kneeling, he prayed. Aloud for the first time in his life. *"Adonai,* I thank you for speaking to my family's heart as you did to my ears two days ago. Such keen agreement as I never dared imagine would come forth. Without protest. I feel I have already been blessed! I go out with great trepidation without the only father I have ever known. You now are my Heavenly *abba*. With whatever little faith that is in me, I will trust you to go with me and my household."

So Abraham, Sarah, Lot, with all their acquired possessions and their entire household bade a tear-filled farewell to their brother and his wife and walked out into the unknown horizon led in simple faith by an audacious promise. Abraham was all of seventy-five years of age when they left for Canaan.

Two

SARAH

What had she been thinking? That another woman's child could be her own? Sarah's happiness over her cleverly devised idea was short-lived. She had under-estimated her Egyptian maid. Misunderstood the insidious female heart. Overlooked Hagar's secretly increasing sneer after Hagar's belly started becoming big. Now the slave-maid had begun strutting. Sarah noticed a stealthy swelling giddiness in the girl, the latter's eyes aglow with a disconcerting pride. A haughtiness of no small measure. A knot began to grow in Sarah's gut. "I'll have to watch the maid more closely," she told herself.

"Sarah, my beloved, what's got into you lately? That black look I see these days mar your beautiful face. Why the sudden sullenness?" Sarah was pleased that dear Abraham noticed her distress. Seizing the opportunity, she confessed, "It was nothing at first, Abraham. When I brought her from Egypt, she was eager to serve me. A good, hard-worker. Trust-worthy. Or so I thought. But now, she despises me."

"Who are you talking about, Sarah? You know you are free to do with your maids as you see fit. You do not need my permission to deal with them." Abraham was puzzled, and not a little irritated. It was quite unlike his wife who was always so confident. Her beauty surpassed her reputation, yes. And her wit and wisdom were well-known by all. Everyone respected and loved her. Who could have caused her such disquiet?

But Sarah took her time and would not come out with the name. Not willingly at first. Instead she wrung her hands in an anxiousness Abraham had never witnessed before. Not even when she had acquiesced to his idea to conceal their real relationship during their time in Egypt. Famine had led them to the land of the Pharaoh. Desperation had led Abraham to conceive the lie to protect himself. And love for her husband had emboldened Sarah to agree to flirt with Pharaoh. Yes, she was a marvel. The quintessential actress. Pharaoh was quickly beguiled by her beauty. Charmed by her uncanny intelligence.

Days passed easier now. Her light olive skin once almost withered by the desert sun now glowed with milky softness. Pharoah liked his women refined, cultured, witty, but submissive. Curved but not fleshy. Preferably virgins. Unblemished and soft to his touch. Cloistered in the opulent palace with the other women being prepared for the Great One, Sarah luxuriated in the daily pampering of warm baths, oiled massages and susinum lotions. The perfume mix of myrrh and cinnamon in balanos oil were distilled by the court's perfumers, hand-picked for their skills in producing olfactory compositions. Food was not scarce inside the opulent palace though the women were careful to feast with an eye to their figures. The famine of the Negev was forgotten as soon as Sarah's stunning beauty, noticed by Pharaoh's officials, landed her in Pharaoh's palace. Only for a second did Sarah wish she was back in that lap of luxury. She had been relieved to have escaped in the nick of time. Rumor had it that Pharaoh had requested her very presence one evening. However, a scream from the eunuch's quarters halted everything. An unruly rash among a few of the girls had turned into oozing pus-filled boils. Recoiling at the sight, court magicians were called in. Superstition trumped science. Someone or something must have angered the gods. Foreigners were first suspects. Incense was burned, furious incantations muttered. Sarah was questioned. Abraham was immediately brought in. Their lie that Sarah was his sister instead of his wife was uncovered. They were instantly banished. But not without Pharaoh's many earlier gifts to win the vivacious Sarah. Arriving meager, they had left Egypt abundant with sheep, cattle, donkeys, camels. Even servants. Sarah, Abraham, his nephew, Lot and their entire household had returned to the Negev enriched.

Partway between Bethel and Ai, Abraham signaled that they should put up their tents there again. Her husband was akin to familiarity more than to change. Here was the place where he had first built an altar to *Yahweh*. Here he would call on the name of the Almighty in thanksgiving for their safety and their unexpected prosperity. But before long, quarreling had set in between their herders. Lot's and Abraham's. Flourishing in Egypt's bounty, the two men had shrewdly done good business in the short time there.

They were now many. Too many to live on the same plot of land without squabbles and constant bickerings. Uncle and nephew knew better than to ignore the almost daily rifts among their people. Separation was the only solution. Amicably they parted ways. Lot and company left. The young man chose to put his roots in Sodom. Abraham and Sarah and their household stayed. Ten years passed like the shepherd's eye blink.

"Ten years, Abraham! You told me the Almighty had spoken to you. Made a promise about children and descendants. Like dust, you said. Uncountable. A covenant you called it. Well, hundreds of moons have passed without even a single child. It wasn't my own idea, you realize, Abraham. Could you blame me for acting upon it finally? Everyone was doing it. Even among our own people. I couldn't stand the whispers of the women any longer. Saana said it was common practice among her people. That's why I was agreeable to it."

"What are you talking about, Sarah? Spit it out, woman!" She was beginning to enter dangerous terrain. Piercing him where it hurt most. Did she not know his own patient anguish? Not hear his night moans? Or realize why he would sit under the great mamre oak alone in silent agony? Querying *Yahweh* with the very same questions himself?

Abraham's rising annoyance stirred Sarah to speak her name. "Hagar", she blurted quickly.

"Hagar? Your Egyptian handmaiden?" Abraham replied, baffled.

"Yes, that Hagar," Sarah repeated the name as if there were others bearing the same name.

"What about 'that' Hagar as you put it, Sarah my dear?"

"This is all your fault, Abraham!" Sarah retorted, catching herself and her husband by surprise. "You are responsible for the wrong I am suffering. I put my maid in your arms, and now that she knows she is pregnant, she despises me. She's become incorrigible. Thinks herself as the mistress now. It's contemptible! I cannot stand for it any longer. May Adonai decide who is right—I or you!" Sarah glowered fiercely at Abraham.

Taken aback, her husband threw up his hands. "She's your servant-maid. Deal with her!" He stormed out of their tent.

Frustrated by her husband's refusal to take responsibility for his part in Hagar's growing disdain for her mistress, Sarah began to treat the maid harshly. With no recourse, Hagar took things into her own hands.

Three

HAGAR

For days she had disappeared into the wilderness. It seemed her life was a series of sudden appearances and disappearances. Abrupt decisions made for her by others. One minute she was in her father's old boat happily helping him fish among the Nile River reeds. The next she was a maid in Pharaoh's harem. Just as she was beginning to settle among the servants in the Waset palace, she was sold into another household. Of the stunningly beautiful Hebrew, Sarah. Then it happened yet again. Abruptly. Uprooted and moved. To a foreign land this time. It seemed like one day she was Sarah's handmaiden, attending to her mistress' personal needs, finally settling into a comfortable routine. But before she knew it, she was in the bed of her master Abraham!

Hagar had never felt so bewildered by the chain of events directing her life. That Sarah had personally coaxed her in the art of pleasuring Sarah's very own husband was something that Hagar had only heard whispered in the seclusion of Pharaoh's female enclave. Never among the women in the Hebrew quarters. At least never before this.

Not too long after she had quietly slid out of Abraham's tent, Hagar found herself revolting at the smell of lamb roasting on the spit of pomegranate wood. She longed for her mother's baba ganoush, the eggplant dip spiced with cumin, parsley, pepper, salt and lemon juice in just a touch of olive oil. Deena, yes, Deena, the old Egyptian slave woman four tents away would have baba ganoush. Not as smooth as made by Hagar's mother, mind you. But enough to quell Hagar's sudden craving.

Hurriedly hitching her long garment, Hagar arrived in front of Deena's goat hair tent. "What brings you here, Hagar?" the old one's voice rang out even before Hagar thought to lift the tent cover. "I can smell another Egyptian from a stone's throw, you know," Deena cackled. "And when was the last time you washed that sorry sight of a garment, by the way? It's a wonder you haven't yet tripped on the embroidered threads hanging off the hems! Mistress Sarah not provide you with her throwaway ones?"

Hagar smiled sheepishly, secretly appeased by the motherly nagging. "Only missing my family, Deena. You're my only true family here now."

"Come, child. Keep an old woman company. It is not everyday that the mistress' handmaiden drops by my tent. Sit. Tell me what's news."

Beckoned inside, Hagar was relieved to be welcomed. Deena was known to be cantankerous sometimes. One never quite knew what to expect with her. Hagar's eyes traveled to the food corner as she entered. "Are you hungry, my dear?" A blush rose so suddenly that it heated Hagar's complexion tincture red. "Would that waft of cumin happen to be baba ganoush perhaps?" asked the hopeful visitor.

"It is, it is! Always a little leftover for another time. Or an unexpected visitor," the wizened one teased.

Hagar was so grateful for familiar company that she stayed chatting with Deena long into the evening. Little did she suspect that the elderly Egyptian woman had once herself been Sarah's handmaiden. Neither did she notice Deena's keen observation as she rose to leave. Nor did she see the latter amble quietly to the mistress' tent soon after. Comfort food had dulled Hagar's usual wariness.

Sarah began to eye her young handmaiden with greater intensity as time rolled by. When Hagar began to appear later and later in the mornings, her mistress cornered her one day. "Late again, Hagar? What's your excuse today?" Sarah queried, hopefully.

"I've not been feeling well lately, mistress Sarah. It's probably nothing." Hagar muttered under her breath.

"Since when did this start, my dear?" Sarah continued trying not to sound too harsh.

"Oh, I don't exactly remember, mistress. Two months, maybe?"

A swift mental calculation razed through Sarah's quick brain. "When was the last time you had your womanly bleed?"

Taken aback by her mistress' directness, Hagar's mind drew a momentary blank. "I can't remember, mistress Sarah. Never been regular with me anyway," she quickly added.

From then on, Hagar began to pay more attention to her menstrual period. But when another month passed and she felt no bloody oozing between her legs, only more nausea and dizziness did a fear begin to take hold of her young heart. How could it be? She had never been in an intimate way with any man before. Except. Except that one time when Sarah had literally pushed her into master Abraham's privacy. The horror of the truth hit Hagar hard. At first. The shame and panic came later. Would she be sent back to Egypt? Her parents would be shamed. No one in that small village would welcome her home. Shunned. She could not utter the word again. It had happened only once before. Hagar had hidden behind the bulrushes as she followed Selima, their neighbor's daughter one starless lonely night. With trembling eyes, she watched Selima slip into the big river. Tears streaming down, the once vibrant teen strode deeper and deeper into the black Nile till she silently disappeared, her once spirited life sucked into the other world by the community shunning. No one said anything the next day or days after. Life continued even as Selima's mother began wandering aimlessly thereafter, muttering her daughter's name to the face of every girl who happened along.

But to Hagar's surprise, she was not sent away. In fact, mistress Sarah began to treat her differently. Kinder. Gentler. No longer making her feel guilty for her tardiness. Even a certain lightness in Sarah's steps could be seen. Even regularly instructing Deena to prepare Egyptian food specifically for Hagar! Then as the moons passed and the reality of what was happening took root in understanding, Hagar's courage emboldened. As her belly grew bigger, the slave girl's head began to swell with potential and possibilities. Why, master Abraham even started asking after her welfare, sometimes in private and more recently even publicly.

Hagar's eyes glowed with pride whenever he came near. She, an Egyptian slave-girl, was carrying the master's child. A surefooted haughtiness could be seen in her steps. She started strutting and ordering the other maids around as if she was the mistress. Daring as well to question Sarah's instructions from time to time. Tensions began to rise between the two females. One trying hard not to reveal her growing regret and anxiety. The other reveling in her new-found status. As Sarah's irritations manifested in bursts of unusual temper, Hagar soon sensed tension between her mistress and master as well.

Four

HAGAR

"So you think you're above me now, slave? Too good to be serving the one who brought you out of your poverty-stricken hovel in your Egyptian village? Parading around in clothes bought by master Abraham, swaggering your protruding belly in our faces?" Sarah's accusations piled with each passing day.

Sarah's gradual change of heart was a revelation to Hagar of the mysterious complexities of the female mind. It was after all Sarah's own idea. Never in her wildest imagination did Hagar ever think it would happen to someone like herself. But then again, had her friends told her that one day she would go from impoverished invisibility to sleeping with an affluent Hebrew foreign master and become the mother of his first offspring, Hagar would have laughed in their faces. Then when the preposterous had actually happened, Hagar's usual timidity grew with a sneering resolve to upend the beautiful Sarah. For what could be more beautiful, more seductive to a childless wealthy man than the young maiden carrying his seed? Yes, in Hagar's mind, she was no longer the maid. She

19

was the esteemed maiden. The fertile one. Some had even whispered that she was fated to be the bearer of Abraham's child. The reality was empowering. Emancipating. So, yes, she had begun to progressively despise Sarah's expectations of continued subservience.

The mistress who had unwittingly led her maid to her husband's tent turned into the vindictive, jealous barren wife. When Hagar's legs started swelling in her fifth month, Sarah demanded more chores from her maid. The latter's complaints of dizziness were only met with accusations of pretext. Confused, Hagar found herself forgetting things. Sarah's displeasures added to Hagar's apprehensions. Life became increasingly unbearable for the maid.

In her desperation, the maid tried to tell master Abraham of his wife's escalating unfair treatment of her. To her disappointment, he only told her to do as bidden. "I have seen pregnant servants do their work without complaining right up to the very time when the baby is coming."

Hagar could not believe what her ears were hearing. master Abraham had been kind and tender with her in bed. Initially, she had cowered before him but his gentleness put her at ease. At the height of his arousal she had felt the strength of his body. Experienced for the very first time the urgency of his desires. Then he trembled in her arms and mouthed incoherent words afterward. Hagar was surprised by passions of her own that she never knew existed. She had looked at the elderly man with disdain and nervousness when she entered his tent. But when he was inside her, she felt she was looking into the very depths of his being. It was an amazing tumult of emotions evoked in the heat of their coupling. Hagar's first sexual encounter left an indelible impression on the young maiden's soul. Then when it was discovered that she was pregnant, master Abraham was ecstatic. Beaming with uncommon joy, she had overheard him thanking mistress Sarah for her magnanimous idea. Smiling to herself, Hagar thought surely master Abraham would take her side. Make Sarah come to her senses. Stop her abuse of the maid bearing the master's heir.

Old Deena had tried to warn Hagar. But Hagar had ignored the signs. Instead, she had arrogantly retorted, "Have no fear, old woman. Once the baby is born, we shall see who will then be Mistress!"

"Naive! Naive girl! Don't say I didn't warn you when the tide turns," Deena scolded.

"All fear and superstition, that's what you are!" Hagar had ungraciously spat out those words.

That was when Hagar put her plan into action and premptively found herself in the desert wilderness. Alone. The food Deena had secretly slipped Hagar before she'd run away was almost all gone. Save for a few dates and a dried piece of bread. The foolishness of her naive behavior was beginning to sink in. What made her think that anyone would come looking for her, much less her owners? She was a slave after all. One of several. Expendable. But Hagar was determined not to turn back.

Day turned into night. Night turned into day. The desert was no respecter of the living. Much less the inexperienced and utterly unprepared. Its beauty and austerity were a deception of its perilous dangers. Those who dare venture forth into desert wilderness unheeding of its menacing hazards will be immensely humbled. Hagar had never before traveled alone. Her move from Egypt through the Sinai had been in the safety of master Abraham's household entourage. Little did she know that the very core of her existence would be tested. By the fifth day, Hagar tasted blood on her cracked lips. She could barely open her eyes, stung shut by the ferocity of yesterday's blinding sandstorm. Her parched throat felt grainy with every intake of breath. For once, Hagar began to fear for the life she was carrying. Her intense hunger was the baby's hunger. Her dying thirst, its dying thirst. Her depleting energy endangered its fragile life. Her arrogant stubbornness, a threat to its very survival.

In the distance, the sound of trickling water drew every ounce left of Hagar's waning strength. Dragging her skinny bulged frame toward the sound, she was ready to drink her last drink and die. The baby within her notwithstanding. She hadn't signed up for this kind of life anyway. Carrier of the master's heir one day. Runaway slave the next. The story of her life. Nothing had changed after all. This was a cruel perplexing world. Why subject the innocent to the same destitution? Better it not enter this heartless world than suffer the indignities of beggary. With this final thought in her mind, Hagar collapsed. A mere hundred yards from a spring.

"Hagar, maid of Sarah, what are you doing here?" A mystifying voice seemed to ask.

Barely able to lift even her pallid face off the unforgiving earth, Hagar heard herself whispering, "H-ow do you know my name? Wh-who are you?"

"I am the one asking the questions, Hagar, maid of Sarah. Where have you come from? And where are you going?" came the irksome queries.

"I'm running away from my mistress Sarah," the maid grudgingly confessed. "Water, please. Whoever you may be, if you are not a hallucination, spare me a sip and let me die," she added.

"Go back to your mistress and submit to her. Remember the child you bear within you," the voice continued unabated.

"Go back?? I will NOT go back to that kind of abuse! Please, just give me a drink. That's all I ask," she persisted.

"Go back, Hagar. For the sake of the new life you carry, submit to your mistress Sarah," demanded the voice. But it was not a severe voice she heard; its strange insistence, unwavering but gentle.

Looking up, Hagar saw first feet. Sandaled. Scuffed by the desert's harshness. Legs, tanned and sanded. The form of a man stood bare inches from where she lay. She felt his strong hands take her weakened limbs. Raise her disheveled body. Enliven her broken spirit.

"Hagar, listen well. I will increase your descendents. They will be too numerous to count." The man's clear voice echoed through the desert expanse. *"You will have a son. Name him 'Ishmael' for the Lord has heard your misery. Your son will be hardy. Strong. Unyielding. Willing anyone and everyone to fight him if they are so inclined. His brothers will not understand his wildness. But he will live to bear many, many sons."*

"Ishmael," Hagar repeated the name. A name she would never have chosen herself. *"Ishmael. Yahweh hears. How apt!"*

The meaning of the name slowly sinking into her befuddled brain. "Yes, I will name him *Ishmael*," she acquiesced as she willed herself to look up again. But silence reigned. The man had disappeared as suddenly as he had appeared.

"I have seen *El Roi,* the Seeing One!" she found herself exclaiming. "Here, between Kadesh and Bered. In this very desert wilderness. This spring, Beer Lachai Roi, it shall be named." With inexplicable resolve, Hagar knelt before the crystal clear waters and quenched her burning throat.

Five

SARAH

Sarah made no attempt to look for her slave girl. As far as she was concerned, her troubles were over. Peace returned to their tent. Until, one day, the runaway trouble returned. Just as mysteriously as she had disappeared, Hagar appeared. Disheveled but strangely no longer distressed. Belly considerably larger. Muttering beneath her breath about *El Roi*. Abraham and Sarah were shocked that the Egyptian servant even knew that Name. He recognized it. Hagar's unnatural peaceful demeanor was disarming. Abraham had the maid moved to her own tent till the baby was born.

Abraham's creased face grinned from ear to ear when a triumphant Sarah brought Ishmael to his long-awaiting arms. Her eyes lit with happiness seeing the eighty-six year old husband of hers cradle the baby in his arms. He was euphoric. Abraham became the doting father. He began to spend all his time with his son. From his very own loins. Hagar had told her master that *El Roi* said to name the child, Ishmael. Because Adonai hears. Adonai had seen her misery. Heard her distressed anxieties. So, Ishmael, he was named.

Ishmael delighted his elderly father. Thrived in his father's undivided attention. Now the slave-son became his father's pride. Prince and heir to the old man's entire wealth, much to Hagar's secret delight and Sarah's mounting regret. "I'll have to watch the boy more closely," Sarah added this reminder to herself. Life was getting more complicated by the day.

But Ishmael could not be watched. His first steps were swift and sure. Nothing like the tentativeness of a first-timer. There was a wild energy in him. Encouraged by his increasingly contemptuous mother, Ishmael grew more wilful with the years. A doting aged father did not help. Arrogance replaced daring insolence. He'd begun to cover up Hagar's manipulations with cunning lies to Sarah's face. Why, in his father's eyes, he could do no wrong!

A despondent thought planted itself in Sarah's mind. What if Abraham's love for his son should turn against her? What if Hagar's illusive dark beauty beguiled him as Ishmael, now a brawny adolescent, had beguiled his father. What if Abraham decided to move Hagar into their tent? "I must open Abraham's eyes to what is happening!" Sarah's agitated mind began churning with unnerving what if's.

Then, one day, Sarah felt different. At first she'd blamed it on the stress over Hagar and Ishmael. Antagonism and arguments were daily occurrences now. The slave girl grew bolder towards her mistress by the hour it seemed. Then when the smell of roasted lamb evoked nausea in her throat, Sarah remembered the strange encounter just months back.

Three foreigners. Dusty feet.

Six

THE VISITORS

From the entrance of his tent under the great mamre trees they had come one noon day. In the increasing heat of the desert sun. Abraham saw them. "Like a mirage against the heat wave," he'd told her later. "I swear they were staring at me, heading for me. Most unnerving." But ever gracious, Abraham had run out to invite the travelers to rest.

"Welcome, Masters, to my humble tent. Let me get some water to cool your feet. Favor me with your presence for a while. My wife will prepare a meal you will never forget," he told the trio. No stranger could resist such hospitality. Not when it came from the heart of the wealthiest man in the region. Not when an offer to refresh their weary bodies came with the offer of a welcome meal. The three men smiled as they slipped off their feet from dusty sandals. Servants had hurried out of nowhere with water to wash.

Abraham disappeared into the tent. "Sarah, visitors! We need your finest bread. Three seahs worth of flour. Knead! Bake! Hurry, woman! They may not be here for long."

Sarah stared at her husband. Easily excitable at the

sight of any visitor. Ever eager for news from afar, she was used to his bursts of social energy. Quickly she turned to organizing the meal. In the distance, Abraham's excited delve into his herd for a choice tender calf could be heard over the din of animals disturbed from their grazing. The servants immediately were abuzz with their master's orders. Soon, a kingly spread of tantalizing lamb stew, fresh milk, curd, and warm baked bread were set before the guests.

Stomachs filled, the men got to chatting. Inclined comfortably on cushions, they asked their host, *"Where is mistress Sarah who graciously prepared this sumptuous meal? We wish to extend our personal gratitude to her kindness."*

"Oh, my dear Sarah is inside the tent," Abraham beamed with pride. "Why, I will be sure to convey your thanks to her, my honored guests. Did I not tell you that she is a marvelous cook?"

"That she is. That she is. But now mark our words, brother Abraham. We will return this time again next year. And Sarah will have a son by then," said one of the three.

"A son, you say?" Abraham could hardly believe his ears. "Ah, that would be a consolation indeed. Long have we dreamed for one of our own. But as you can see, kind masters, I am what you would say 'past my prime'? And Sarah is no spring chicken either!" Abraham chuckled at his own jibe. "But I do have a son already. Ishmael. A strapping teenager. Strong like his old man. Handsome with the dark beauty of his Egyptian mother. Sarah's handmaiden." Abraham quickly added.

"No, no, no! I am not talking about the boy of your maid, master Abraham. Sarah's, and Your son is what I'm saying,"

insisted the same voice. At that, a distant snicker was heard behind the tent.

Hiding behind, Sarah had overheard the entire conversation. "I am old, and so is my lord; am I to have pleasure again?" she thought to herself. "Such a ridiculous notion!" Instantly, the man turned to Abraham. *"Why did Sarah laugh and ask, 'Am I really going to bear a child when I am so old?' Is anything too hard for Adonai? At the time set for it, at this season next year, I will return to you; and Sarah will have a son."* His insistent reiteration was disconcerting.

Stepping from her hiding, Sarah timidly revealed herself before her husband's surprised eyes. "I did not laugh,' she lied.

"O yes, indeed you did laugh, Sarah. But you'll see. This time next year, it will be a different kind of laughter when we visit your tent again. Adonai never forgets his promise." With this, the strangers rose to their feet, clasped her husband's hands in farewell, and walked out from the tent, leaving their hosts bewildered.

Sarah's mind returned from her musing. It seemed a lifetime ago. Now little Isaac lay in her arms. Indeed, her unbelieving peal of laughter at the mysterious trio's revelation had turned into an incredulous burst of resounding joy at the miraculous birth of her son. *Their* son. Somehow Abraham's shriveled seed had taken inside her very own sagged barren womb and formed a new life. In their dotage. An impossibility had taken place. It had happened just as the three peculiar visitors had insisted. Their uncanny prediction had turned prophetic.

Tomorrow would be the feast of Isaac's weaning. Sarah had seen the mockery of her precious boy's half-brother, Ishmael. Had heard his unholy sniggering among his group of teenagers. Noted the wary jealousy of his slave mother. Two different worlds colliding. Two different seeds must be separated. Hagar and her boy must go.

Seven

ISAAC & REBEKAH

The old man had come leading a caravan of ten camels. Not two, or five, but ten. Each ship of the desert fully dressed. Colorful tapestries of woven animal hair adorned the camel backs. The saddles were tanned leather. Quite obviously loaded with some valuable cargo too. But the leader had the demeanor of an *eved,* a servant. Old, his eyes displayed the humble wisdom gained from experience. He had the camels kneel down near the well. Talking to himself, his eyes shut, the wrinkles on his furrowed forehead dancing in tandem with his silent words. Fascinating. From afar, Rebekah watched and wondered where the master was.

With her jar on shoulder, Rebekah headed toward the village well, trying to tread as quietly as possible. Eliezer's light ears however picked out approaching sandaled footsteps. Most definitely female. Opening his eyes, he saw her even before he had finished his prayer. Her simple beauty accentuated in the evening desert light. Remembering his specific earnest prayer of a breath ago, Eliezer decided to test the waters immediately.

"Shalom, kind maiden, would you please let down your jug and allow a weary traveler to have a little drink?" he politely asked.

Kindly, he heard her say, "Drink, sir," as she let down her jug and gave him a drink. And when she had finished giving him a drink, she said, "I will draw for your camels also, until they are done drinking." Rebekah emptied her jug into the trough, ran back to the well, and drew for all his camels.

At this Eliezer almost choked in excitement. Without saying a word, he watched her closely to learn whether or not the Lord God of his master Abraham had made his journey successful.

"Thank you," Eliezer continued. "Please accept this token of appreciation for your kindness." He took out a gold nose ring weighing a beka and two gold bracelets weighing ten shekels from one of the several chests on the camels. "May I be so bold to ask whose daughter you are? And is there room in your father's house for us to spend the night?"

Surprised by his generous gifts, Rebekah answered Eliezer, "I am the daughter of Bethuel, the son that Milkah bore to Nahor." And, yes, most definitely." she added. 'We have plenty of straw and water for your camels, as well as room for you to spend the night."

To her utter amazement, the *eved* instantly bowed down exclaiming, "Blessed be *Adonai*, who has not abandoned his kindness and faithfulness to my master, Abraham. As for me, the Lord has led me on the journey to the house of my master's relatives!"

Rebekah ran. Bolted. Breathless, she narrated the strange encounter to her mother's household. As soon as he had seen the nose ring, and the bracelets on his sister's arms and heard Rebekah tell what the man had said to her, Laban, her brother, went out to the man and found him standing by the camels near the spring.

"Welcome, you who are blessed," he said. "Welcome! I will have a place prepared for you and your tired camels to rest the night."

A still stunned Eliezer followed Laban to the house as the camels were unloaded. Straw and fodder were brought for the camels, and water for him and his men to wash their feet. Then food was set before him, but he said, "I will not eat until I have told you what I have to say."

That was how Rebekah was introduced to the name Isaac. At the thought of her husband, a smile momentarily lit upon her face. Isaac—kind, gentle, and most definitely handsome—had for many passages of the moon just been a name mentioned by her grandfather Nahor. Not without great reverence and awe, mind you. Isaac, the promised, long-awaited 'son of the Covenant'. The one whose conception was improbable, impossible. Why, his own parents were 'the venerable aged' by the time he made his appearance! To bear a child for the very FIRST time in her ninetieth year??!! Unreasonable. Unfathomable. Impossible. Insane.

Yes, when Rebekah first laid eyes upon Isaac he had been out in the fields, meditating. 'Hmmm...a thinking man,' she mused to herself, "unlike my rowdy brothers. Certainly, nothing like loud, brash Laban!" She instinctively uncovered her face, letting her veil slide ever so subtly from head to shoulder like her mother had taught her. Sensing her shyness, Isaac quickly turned to Eliezer instead but not without noticing his beloved mother's gold bracelets on Rebekah's slender arms and the beka-worth gold nose ring. Wise, faithful Eliezer's gleaming face told it all. Mission accomplished! But Isaac let the old servant tell his story. Listening to the unfolding tale of God's clear guidance, Isaac's amusement soon gave in to the latter's rising excitement. Chuckles turned to hilarity to uproarious laughter as Eliezer's hands gestured with amazing agility in his tale of wonder.

Heart bursting with thankfulness at *Yahweh's* answer to their prayers, Isaac held out his hands to his young bride and led her to his mother's tent. His love for her was so instant, so dizzying. It had shaken Isaac and Rebekah to the core. Now they understood the intimacy of his parent's perfect match. Quiet Isaac finally found comfort after his beloved mother's death.

Wistfully, Rebekah recalled the night of their union. He had led her unhurriedly into his mother's tent. Undressed her tenderly, his eyes stayed on hers. Nothing like what her *imma* had taught her to expect. He was wealthy yet unspoilt. Waited on hand and foot by his entire household, yet undemanding. Considerate and courteous, his strong arms had laid her gently on the floor of their wedding tent. Closing his eyes, Isaac drank in the fragrance of his virgin bride. The years of waiting would be patiently disciplined till she was ready. Rebekah's secret fear melted away, his tender touch awakening a boldness inside she never knew existed. Aroused, he sank into her freshness, his love sweeping over them like a tidal wave. And Rebekah would grow to love her new husband more and more with each passing day.

Eight

TWINS: JACOB & ESAU

It seemed in life he was always late. Or later. Born the younger of twins. Emerged from womb-to-world grasping his brother's heel. As if not to be left behind in their mother's amniotic sac. It seemed life was forever a struggle. From conception to birth, a battle. The brothers had fought, albeit playfully, even in that safe bodily cocoon. Space for one body within that female enclave meant a constant maneuvering between the two. For the most comfortable position, the strategic spot for feeding, the roomiest corner for ever-growing limbs. But no matter how much they wriggled and wrangled, the older by twenty seconds was stronger. So Esau emerged first. Red, ruddy, glowing to the oohs and aahs of the midwives and to the utter delight of the father, Isaac, beaming proudly.

But he, Jacob, would not be overlooked. Clinging tightly to his brother's heel, the younger made his entrance known. He would NOT be ignored. His tenacity made their mother smile. Small. Determined. Feisty. A spooky apparition of herself. Rebekah loved Jacob at first sight.

No twins could be more mismatched. That was their genesis—divergently distinct. Jacob had heard his mother recount their fetal jostling. A thousand times over. Initial delight becoming irritating discomfort, her pregnancy, an endless heaving internal baby battle. Their growing protrusions, a source of embarrassment. Her coveted sleep, a substantial illusion. Till eyes an insomniac glaze and her spirit depleted of strength, she sought Adonai in desperation. And she was told words that no mother should ever have to hear.

"Two nations in your womb. Rivals from birth. One will be stronger than the other. The older will serve the younger."

Rebekah kept these other-worldly words to herself. Watching. Wondering. Watching to see if they were prophetic. Willing them to be wrong. Wondering if anything could be done to undo the augury. But as the boys grew, play would turn from innocent to manipulative. Name-calling (a favorite of Esau's), from teasing to tearful badgering. Isaac cheered the older son's manliness, Rebekah defended the younger's reticence. Esau loved his brother as long as they both knew who was the leader. Jacob adored Esau but with measured wariness. The hunter always returned from his hunting triumphant and loud. Eyes riveted to their father's applause, Esau would hurl his game on the floor for all to see. "Brother, busy your hands with the cooking. Make haste the meal with your womanly skills. Father and I are hungry as you can tell. A feast tonight, brother. My trophy, your culinary masterpiece!"

Eager to acquiesce, Jacob and Rebekah would summon the servants. The prey was soon skinned. Meat and bones, sinew and tendons pried apart and tenderized. This was their favorite time together in the kitchen. Mother and son scheming recipes, teaching and learning, experimenting and laughing. Till a meal fit for the palace wafted its way onto the dining plates. Ingested with gusto, Isaac's satisfaction would burp a mirthful sound to the family. The pattern continued. Played itself into familiarity. Until. Until familiarity began to breed a sinister envy. The younger one grew hungry. Hungry for their father's approval. Applause for himself for once. Dissatisfied with playing second fiddle, a plan began to seed in his culinary brain. One so simple its deviousness would surely be undetectable. Jacob decided to test it the next time his hunter brother came home with his kill.

Rabbit. Lamb. Goat. Deer. Squirrel… Esau loved his meat. Like Isaac. Nothing was relished more by father and son than wild game seasoned with fresh aromatic herbs and spices sizzling over the open fire on a spit. Jacob had heard Esau leave with his friends before first light. The dawn of hunting season did that. Roused men from their ennui. In his younger years Jacob too had been caught up in the excitement of the sport. Tagged along with his brother and their friends. Eager to be part of the group. But he could not summon any euphoria for the pursuit. Nor the kill. Turning prey to palatable heaven? Now that was a different pursuit altogether. That was where Jacob's innate juices awakened.

Day one seldom rewarded the eager hunters with triumph. Jacob knew that from years of observation. They would return rowdy with talk. A rabbit or two in hand. Infrequently a deer. But always famished. Jacob knew exactly what brew to tantalize Esau's growling stomach with. He would concoct a lamb stew so divine with potatoes and carrots so sweet that his twin would not think twice except to dig into the meal directly. Concoctions. Yes, the younger brother was adept at that. Having learned from watching his beloved mother. Listened to her schemes to get him his beloved father's favor from time to time. Now as he cooked, Jacob's brain turned to concocting his most daring scheme yet.

Birthright. Jacob longed for his twin's birthright. The endless dreams he had had in which he had been born first. Ahead of Esau. Esau to whom everything came easy. Looks. Strength. Skill. Favor. Adulation from father and the girls alike. Esau who never had to work hard for anything. Who delighted in challenging the norm and getting away with it. Always. Esau had no inkling of his favored position. Took his rights for granted. His lackadaisical attitude toward life was as profane as his handsome good looks. What was his brother's right of birth alone Jacob would possess by trade. A legitimate business transaction. A shrewd deal. Nothing untoward. And his brother would not know it till it was too late. That would be how the younger would fulfill the prophecy given at their mother's pregnancy. After all, was it not true that the fittest survived in this world? Except in this case, it would be the fittest of mind and not of brawn that would be the victor.

First, Jacob carefully deboned the lamb shoulders. Trimming only a little fat before cutting them into chunks. The lentils were already soaking in the pot. Rebekah always had spices already ground—cumin, coriander, fennel and pepper. He mixed in a handful with olive oil coating the meat together well with salt and onion coarsely chopped. In his favorite earthen pot, garlic and potatoes simmered in bone broth. This he carefully poured over the lamb and onions, threw in a few rosemary sprigs, and left to cook in its cover. For three hours while the lamb stewed Jacob turned his attention to setting the scene.

Three hours. In that time Jacob's mind swung back and forth like a pendulum. Memories of their childhood flashed. Games played between the brothers. Happy moments. Twin thoughts. One knowing what the other would do next. Shared psyche. Smidgens of innocent sibling joy that almost led Jacob to abandon his careful plan to outwit the other. They were brothers after all. Of the same mother. One father. Then that glint of favoritism in their father's eyes for Esau. That secret shared intimacy between the two, at times subtle, but more often blatant. Jacob had seen it. Sensed it. Felt it. Those incidents cratered a hole of hurt so deep in Jacob's heart that all thoughts of abandoning his appetizing ploy ceased. Enough of vacillating! Jacob chided himself. Isaac was growing old. Time was of the essence. Sentiments would only ruin his future.

He would have to master the speech and speed needed to beguile his ravenous brother. So engrossed was he in the fragile matter that he almost forgot to mash the soaking lentils or add in fresh leeks! But, no matter. Jacob had everything in control. By the time Esau's footsteps made themselves known, the savory aroma had pervaded their tent. Jacob's smile was as welcoming as his bubbling red lamb stew.

The exchange was swift. The deception so guileless it astounded even the perpetrator. Jacob could not have planned it any better. Though for a split second he almost second-guessed its success. Esau not fully realizing what he had relinquished until it was too late. O, the delight of it elicited a satisfied smile on Jacob's face. He rubbed his shoulders, sore from hours of cooking. However his elation lasted only till his head hit his pillow that night. Dread crept over his being. What had he done? To his very own twin! Why had he done it? Why had his desire for his brother's birthright become a yearning so profound that it seared a hole in his soul? Mysterious in its fervor Jacob would wrestle with this quandary for the rest of his life. Fear slithered like a leech, silently creeping over his body, sucking the initial exhilaration out of his palpitating heart. What if Esau divulged his brother's trickery to their father? Would Isaac disown Jacob? Banish him from the family like he deserved? Jacob tossed and turned through the night. Cold sweat drenched his bed. He awoke engulfed in shame like a child from his bed-wet.

Esau awoke the next morning glutted with yesterday's pleasures. The hunt had been fun. Unproductive but great fun. First hunt of the season was always that way. Eyes lazy from ease needed to be trained again. Senses dulled by play required sharpening. Flaccid muscles cried for toughening. He and his friends had ventured out just far enough from their village into the desert wilderness to claim that the hunt had begun for them. Far and long enough into the day to stir up their stomach juices for food. Instinct told

Esau that his twin would be hovering over the fire. Just as creeping stealthily up to hover over an unsuspecting kill excited him, his brother was somehow aroused by thoughts of preparing exquisite meals. Strange this womanish delight. Esau could never understand that innate difference between them. Nevertheless his musing was quickly banished by the rumblings in his belly upon their return from the day's hunt. But this time somehow Jacob was reluctant to readily serve up his brew. He had wanted something for his work. It was a game they had often played as boys. Something for something. Nothing for nothing. Famished, Esau was eager to play along. So, his brother wanted his birthright. What use was that to a starving man anyways? Unaware of Jacob's cunning, Esau dug into the appetizing serving. Slurped every bit of deliciousness in it, belched a fulfilled belch of contentment, slapped his domesticated brother's back, and off he headed to his rest.

But after Esau's mind was cleared from his nocturnal slumber, he realized the recklessness of his easy surrender. Understood the sly of the younger. Cognizance of his own foolishness and his twin's ingenuity shamed Esau into silence. For now he would suppress the rising anger at himself and at his sibling. He would find a way to trap Jacob into returning his stolen birthright. Somehow. His mind was set on it. And once Esau's mind was set on something, nothing would get in his way. Nothing.

The opportunity presented itself unexpectedly. Aged Isaac had sent for him early one morning. Before sunup faithful Eliezer had stood outside Esau's tent, whispering

"*Esav, Esav*, master *Yitz'chak* is calling for you. Your father seems agitated. Says to make haste but come on the quiet."

What propitious timing! Esau took it as a sign of the gods' displeasure with Jacob's duplicity. Now would be his revenge on his brother. Not that Esau cared too much for his father's religion. Or anything spiritual for that matter. No, he had little regard for that nonsense. But to be hoodwinked, duped by his own twin? That was altogether different. Unthinkable! Esau would not be outwitted. Nobody will make a laughing stock of him. He would show that rogue who had both brawn AND brains. Throwing on the cloak his father had given him not too long ago, he hurried to Isaac's tent.

"*Esav*, is that you, my son?" the old man called out when he heard footsteps entering.

"Yes, father, it is I, *Esav*." His father always referred to them by their Hebrew names. "I came as fast as Eliezer told me."

"Ah *Esav, my Esav!* It is good to have you near. My eyes are as dim as I am old. *Yahweh* alone knows when my days on this earth are done. But my belly is not yet past its craving for some wild meat. Get your quiver and arrows. Go hunt in the open country where the best game is. Have it prepared the way you and I like it. I yearn to savor every morsel of it together with my beloved son before I lay down my head forever. And I will give you my blessing then."

Esau's hidden wrath against his sibling was erased. Instantly. By the hankering of their elderly father for some earthy game. And the old man's desire to bless his firstborn. What sheer luck! There was no need to plan a ruse after all.

It was to be handed to him on a platter. As it should be. He was and always would be Number 1 son. No wile of Jacob will rob Esau of that right.

"Yes, *abba*, I will hunt for you. Perchance the gazelle you so favor. We will have a feast, you and I, upon my return. A feast fit for the blessing of your firstborn!" Esau enthused.

"Shhh, *Esav*. Not so loud. Your mother does not yet know of my intentions. And there is no need to tell her or anyone until it's done. Let it be a surprise. It will be our little secret. For now. Go, quick, my son. Before it gets too late. This old man may not be able to hold on to such a secret for too long. Go! Go! And hurry back!"

Delighted with the trust his father had placed on him, Esau scurried out of the tent. He would have proudly invited his friends on this the most providential of all hunts. But Isaac had sworn him to secrecy. And this was one secret Esau was eager to keep. He could not wait to see the look of dismay and disappointment on his twin's face when the table was turned on him! Without further ado, Esau stole toward his own tent for his hunting gear, soundlessly got on his mount and headed into the wilderness.

Nine

REBEKAH

Rebekah slid away from behind the tent she shared with Isaac. Her suspicions had at once been aroused when she had seen gray-haired Eliezer shuffling out early that morning. Her husband's servant was nothing but faithful to his beloved master Abraham's son. Old as he was now, Eliezer was never too old to do Isaac's bidding. Amazingly light and quick still on his feet despite his bent back. Her keen eyes followed his moving form to Esau's tent. Her eldest son's immediate appearance hot on the servant's arrival alerted her attention further. Something was definitely afoot. Rather than enter and interrupt the rendezvous, Rebekah decided to listen in from outside. She knew what Esau's quick temper could induce. What was her increasingly senile husband of a man up to with his favored son?

Unnerved by what she'd heard, Rebekah almost staggered into their tent to confront her husband. What had become of the good, gentle *Yitz'chak* she knew? They had shared a long, loving marriage of trust. No secrets separated them.

Except for their open secret of favoring each of their sons. The audacity of him to go behind her back! Did he not remember Adonai's will expressed to her before the twin's birth? Did he think to thwart the Lord's plans? Foolishness! Foolishness! Old age must have addled his brain. Disappointment and distress contended for clarity. She had to do something to circumvent that underhanded conspiracy between father and son.

"*Ya'akov, Ya'akov,* where are you, my dearest son?" Rebekah yelled as she charged into Jacob's tent, flabbergasted.

"In here, mother. Just finished my breakfast. You're up early. Here, have some goat cheese. Made them myself last night." Jacob replied.

"No time for eating, Ya'akov. Listen! I heard your father telling your brother, 'Bring me game, and make it tasty so I can eat it. Then I will give you my blessing in the presence of *Adonai,* before my death.'" Rebekah blurted out the disastrous news.

Jacob's hand froze in mid-air, the soft cheese in transit to his mouth. "Who told you this, mother?" he asked, hoping it was a mere rumor.

"Nobody, Ya'akov. I heard it with my own ears. This very morning. Outside your father's tent."

"You were eavesdropping? Why? It's your tent too. You have every right to be with your husband." Jacob stated, a little confused.

"Rushing. Rushing. First Eliezer. Then that brother of yours. I sensed something amiss. Always up to no good, *Esav* is. He can beguile your father's mind just like that as you know. His maneuvers, smooth and sweet, like his tongue and looks." Poor Rebekah's mind was scuttling to formulate a plan as fast as her lips were spilling the beans to Jacob.

"Slow down, mother. Are you sure you heard correctly? Father knows the prophecy. 'The elder shall serve the younger.' Clearly the blessing is mine. Besides, *Esav* has already bargained away his birthright. To me!"

"What? Given his birthright away, you say? When?" Rebekah could not believe her ears.

"Last week. And no, he didn't *give it away*, as you put it. Though we both know he has no regard for it. Except for freely flinging away to one and all his boast with women, wine, and sport, my brother gives nothing for nothing. No, mother. I *negotiated* for it. Cleverly, if I may say so myself."

"Fair and square," he continued. "My delectable lamb stew to sate his gluttonous appetite for his unappreciated birthright. It was incredibly easy! You should have been there, mother." Jacob smiled as he relayed the story for the first time. His mother would understand. She had always known how much he valued the spiritual. He had inherited grandfather Abraham's high regard for *Yahweh* from forever.

"Well, all that will be for naught when *Esav* returns from his hunt. Now pay attention to me, my son, and do what I tell you. Go to the flock, and bring me back two choice kids. I will make it tasty for your father, the way he likes it; and you will bring it to your father to eat; so that he will give his blessing to you before he knows it. Hurry! There is no time to lose if you want to have your father's blessing, Ya'akov!"

"But mother, father will not so easily be fooled. *Esav* is hairy. My skin is smooth. A touch will instantly give me away. Then father's curse will be upon me instead!" The very thought of it sent a chill down Jacob's spine.

"You think I have not already considered all that, Ya'akov? Stop quibbling with me. Has your mother ever lied to you? Go get me the young goats. Do as I tell you. Let your father's curse be on me if this goes wrong. Just go, quick. Now, I say!!" Without any more words, Rebekah pushed Jacob out on his critical errand, the plot thickening as urgently as the shove she gave him.

"O *Yitz'chak, Yitz'chak*, what are you thinking?" Rebekah muttered to herself as her hands rummaged for the necessary spices for the decisive meal. "Why the secrecy? This complicity with *Esav*?" The sheer connivance of it was bewildering. Beyond the usual gentle meekness of the faithful *Yitz'chak* she had known all their lives together. Perhaps that very meekness was the culprit. Where Rebekah was outspoken and forthright, Isaac preferred negotiating to confrontation. Opposites attract, it is said. Jacob was like his father in this sense. Introverts veered toward pondering and contemplation, musings and meditations. In direct contrast to Esau's penchant for the outdoors and sometimes lewd outbursts of temper. Perhaps in his advanced age an underlying fear of incurring the wrath of his firstborn now lurked in Isaac.

Rebekah had to move quickly. There was no time for slow-cooking today, not if she wanted to beat Esau and Isaac at their own scheming. "Oh, where is my precious saffron? I hope Jacob has not used all of it for his 'brotherly' stew!" Between pepper and paprika, salt and vinegar, beans and potatoes, garlic and cumin, Rebekah's mind was churning.

Her body was almost trembling with the complexity of devising a foolproof strategy and his favorite meal at the same time.

"No open blessing ceremony as it ought to be? A covert one instead? Am I not your wife? The mother of our sons?!" Her soliloquy continued as she prepared to cook once Jacob returned. "Do you think this will undermine *Adonai's* will? Think of your brother Yishma'el! Have you not learned the lesson of your *imma* Sarah and *abba* Abraham taking things into their own hands?" She continued. When she was a child, her brother Laban had often teased her about her perceptiveness. Calling her *'Resolute Rebekah'*. She had hated Laban's teasing and had watched his clever but sometimes insidious exploitations of people with indignation. Never for a minute did Rebekah stop to consider that her very present actions were a contradiction to her own reflections. That she would resolve to 'help' *Yahweh* fulfill his purpose for her children revealed her own lack of confidence in the Almighty. She was only mindful of the divine words given to her during her pregnancy with the twins. As the boys grew, she had watched with not a little anxiety the unfolding of all four of their lives, each intertwining inevitably with the others. It was her resourcefulness that had kept the men in her life at peace within the family.

When Jacob finally returned, Rebekah's plan was already in full swing. In her brain. He only had to be in concurrence with it. His very inheritance was at stake. She could not see why he would disagree.

"O good, you've slaughtered the animal. I will make your father's favorite goat meat pepper soup, and barley bread."

"You've already made the bread, mother? And hummus as well? I could smell the garlic roasted grain as I came near." Jacob enthused, swallowing down a glob of saliva. He had almost forgotten the reason for this meal.

"Ya'akov, leave this cooking to me. Go get me your brother's tunic. Fortunately I did the washing just yesterday. Put it on. Make sure that goat skin tunic covers over your neck and arms. That should be hairy enough." Rebekah ordered. "It is a good thing your father's eyes are not as keen now. The smell of the stew will hopefully combine with Esau's clothes to replicate your brother's body's scent!"

Jacob was amazed by his mother's inventiveness. Her determination was inspiring once her mind was set on something. He had always loved that about Rebekah. Her protective spirit over him was, well... indefatigable. Yes, that was the word for her. He shook his head as he practiced wearing Esau's clothes. Thankfully their voices sounded almost exactly the same. His was only a tweak higher. But only his mother and the nurse-maid were the two people who could readily tell the difference. Looking at himself in his twin's garb, Jacob could not believe that their mother would herself plot against her husband's own wishes. He had been reluctant to share his own manipulation for Esau's birthright earlier with Rebekah for fear she would be aghast. But this very expedient and dangerous undertaking of hers brought a new appreciation of her love for her younger son. Tenacious. If he had had but a small measure of her *chutzpah,* all this jostling for his father's blessing would have been much, much easier.

The aroma of his mother's cooking brought Jacob back from his reverie. He had known that the day would come for the matter of the blessing of the firstborn. His anxiety about this increased with each passing year, each aging of his beloved father. The man he admired most in his life. How that prophecy would play out Jacob had no idea. He could only conceive that its fulfillment would either be by the early demise of his older brother, or by a twist of meandering events. The former was unlikely, especially given Esau's robust health. That their mother herself was earnest in securing the blessing for him convinced Jacob of the rightness of the latter. It was time for the daring deed.

Ten

ISAAC

As Isaac lay in bed awaiting the return of Esau from his hunting, his mind turned to the matter at hand. It wasn't that he had entered his second childhood (as some, including his family, had been insinuating in recent years) yearning for the game meat of his youth. Of late though he did find himself craving. Craving for the simple carefree days. When life had been fun playing with his brother. Half-brother notwithstanding. When Ishmael was the apple of their father's eye. And Isaac's hero. At fourteen, Ishmael was already as sharp an archer as you could find. How Isaac had looked forward to Ishmael teaching him how to hold the bow, hunt the mountain lion. Man stuff. Esau was much like his uncle Ishmael. Tall, confident, skilled, bold, unconstrained. Isaac hadn't minded his brother's brazenness. Not at all. He had actually admired that. Secretly wished one day to grow up to be as daring and dashing. Like his big brother.

But Sarah's paranoia had won. First Ishmael and his mother, Hagar the maid, had been sent away, "Never to share in the inheritance of my son." Sarah had declared.

Isaac had refused to refer to Ishmael as 'half-brother'. A sibling was a sibling, no matter how much or how little. The same blood coursed through their veins. Sarah thought him naive. Abraham quietly lauded him for this. But their lives were never the same again after the families were separated. Isaac became the center of his parent's life. Yes, his birth had brought consummation to the deep longing in their hearts. Laughter had replaced years of patient waiting. And put the village gossip to rest. Isaac, the favored son, could do no wrong. He was the fulfillment of a covenant. But life became lonely. Being waited on hand and foot was no substitute for boyhood adventuring with brothers and peers. Isaac felt the burden of covenant-keeping. He vowed never to repeat his parent's mistake of sending his only brother away.

Esau had the right of blessing as the first born. That was the tradition. Isaac was not about to balk time-honored traditions. He had personally seen the tragic shock of abandonment of Ishmael by their father. Ishmael, his very own flesh and blood. The blessing of the first-born cruelly wrenched away. Given to the younger instead, leaving Isaac with guilt and sadness and unanswered questions. He had also experienced the isolation of great expectations laid upon his shoulders from birth. So Isaac had been tender towards his own sons. Especially so to the older. Esau had been given the freedoms Isaac never had. Freedom from responsibilities Isaac had not asked for and was adamant not ever to put on Esau. No, he was NOT going to deprive Esau of his birthright and blessing, regardless of Rebekah's assertions.

Moreover, there had been no covenant about Jacob owning his brother's blessing. As far as Isaac was concerned

Rebekah was the only one who insisted on that. Said she had inquired of *Adonai*. Had been told of two nations in her womb. Rivals they would become. The older would serve the younger. Isaac had stared at his beautiful Rebekah in shock. She had become more ravishing in her pregnancy. But the child-bearing months were arduous. Her back had been racked with incessant pains and wearisome jostlings. The birthing of the twins was grueling. Perhaps the intense labor had confounded her mind? The initial joy of becoming first-time parents was exhilarating. Twin sons. Twice blessed! Double elation! Over the years Isaac and Rebekah watched the growth of their sons with the utmost devotion, wondering at the boys' similarities, puzzling over their differences. Rebekah repeatedly hovering over shy Jacob, Isaac taking great pleasure over boisterous Esau. Isaac smiled to himself as he reflected on his life as a father. Jacob will understand once Isaac explained the reasons for his action. That is what Isaac assured himself. *Adonai* will provide for Jacob. Just as his own father, Abraham, had explained to Isaac that momentous day at Moriah.

"Where are you going, *abba*?" Isaac had asked, watching Abraham saddling his donkey early one morning.

"You'll see, my son. Come, this is one journey we are to make together. You and I, father and son."

Delighted to be invited along, Isaac had hurried to dress for the mysterious journey while the two servants loaded cut wood on his father's donkey. No one rode the animal. They walked. And walked. And walked. The mystery thickened by the hour. Three days. Patiently trudging alongside his father, speaking only when spoken to. Three days quietly trusting that *abba* knew where he was heading. What he was being about. Then just as abruptly, Abraham's eyes had lifted high. Up to a mountain. Just when Isaac had hoped that they had arrived at their destination, his father turned to the two servants and said, "Stay here with the donkey. I and the boy will go there. We will worship and return to you."

'Oh, that's why we are going. To worship *Adonai* on the mountain where He has often met with *abba*." Isaac now understood. His heart beat a little faster. Perhaps he too will get to meet with *Yahweh*!

Before anyone could say a word, Abraham took the wood for the burnt offering and placed it on Isaac. He himself carried the flint and the knife. As the two of them went on together, Isaac spoke up and said to his father Abraham, *"abba?"*

"Yes, my son?" Abraham replied.

"The fire and wood are here," Isaac said, "but where is the lamb for the burnt offering?"

"God will provide the lamb for a burnt offering, my son," his father had replied. They walked on together.

When they reached the mountain top, Isaac had helped his father build an altar. He had never seen Abraham do this before, build an altar to *Yahweh*. Only heard the stories of his *abba's* personal encounters with the Lord. At Shechem, between Bethel and Ai, and at Hebron. Worship and sacrifice, the heart of each encounter. Abraham moved with focus, piling stone upon stone with precision. Unhewn stones, every single one handpicked with purpose. Then the wood was laid meticulously upon the stones, piece by piece. It was poetry in motion. A sacred experience.

Then, shockingly, Isaac found himself bound, hand and foot by his father. And laid upon the wood. On the altar. Horrific realization seized Isaac. *He* was the sacrifice!! How could *abba* do such a thing? Did he not teach them that human sacrifice was an abomination to *Yahweh?* How can he, Isaac, the promised son, be offered up like an animal before he could even taste life's promises? Has *abba* in his devoted piety lost his sanity? Isaac struggled to make sense of what was happening. But Abraham's strong left hand held him down. He saw *abba* reach out his right hand, take the knife from its sheath raising it high to slay his son. His one and only son. The long-awaited promised Son of the Covenant. Isaac shut his eyes to face the atrocity.

Without warning, a voice rang out through the misty mountain. *"Abraham! Abraham!"*

"Here I am," Abraham replied. Strange how he knew that voice.

"Do not lay a hand on the boy," the voice said. *"Do not do anything to him. Now I know that you fear me, because you have not withheld from me your son, your only son."*

Abraham raised his eyes and looked, and there behind him was a ram caught in the thicket by its horns. Stunned by the change of instructions, he released his grip on Isaac, freed the ram from the bush entanglement and promptly tied the animal by its legs. Turning to Isaac, Abraham sliced the ropes binding his son. Isaac tumbled off the altar, astounded beyond words. The ram was offered up as a burnt offering in his place. Abraham called the place *Adonai* Yir'eh, *Adonai* provides. Isaac secretly called the place 'My Escape!'

As the events of his life flashed before his dim eyes, Isaac prayed *Adonai* would once again provide. Provide Esau with appreciation for the legacy of his birth inheritance once he received the blessing of the first-born. Provide Jacob with understanding of his birth position as the second son. Provide Rebekah with her willing support of her husband's deed. And provide Isaac with sweet peace in his waning last days in this world.

Eleven

REBEKAH & JACOB

"Make haste, Jacob! There is no time to lose. Esau will be back before we know it." Rebekah steeled her voice to remain as steady as the hands that held out the steaming bowl of her husband's favorite goat stew and the bread baked just the way she knew he liked it. Their eyes met. Jacob's and his mother's. A split second of trepidation and doubt passed like an eely current between them.

"Are you sure this will work, mother?" Jacob reiterated.

"Trust me, Jacob. It will. Trust yourself and all will be well." Rebekah assured her son. She was just as anxious to see their subterfuge through but this was not the time for any misgivings. Irresolution spelt only doom. She pushed Jacob out with a resolve and a reminder, "Speak as your brother would. Sweeten your *abba's* heart the way Esau always does with his boasts. *Abba Yitshack's* shaky hands may reach out to touch yours. Decrepit with age as we may think, his mind is far from tottering yet. Be subtle but swift," she warned.

Jacob inhaled a cavernous breath. And walked to Isaac's tent.

He went to his father and said, *"Abba."*

"Yes, my son," Isaac answered. "Who is it?"

"Esav, abba, your firstborn. I have done as you told me. Please sit up and eat some of my game, so that you may give me your blessing as you promised."

"You're back already, *Esav?* Isaac asked. "How did you find it so quickly, my son?"

"Adonai gave me success, father. I could not believe my good fortune. Perhaps it is a sign. It is a happy day for us both. Here, take a whiff of the spicy aromas, *abba."* Jacob replied.

"It smells sensational!" Isaac said to Jacob, "But first come near so I can touch you, my son, to know whether you really are my son *Esav* or not."

Jacob went close to his father, willing his booming heart to quieten underneath his disguise.

Isaac touched him and said, "The voice is the voice of *Ya'akov,* but the hands are the hands of *Esav."*

Jacob extended his goat skinned hand further out. His father's hands reached up to the arms. He felt the pileous skin. Wanting to be absolutely sure, he pressed into the outstretched arms and felt for the muscles below.

Isaac did not recognize his younger son for his hands were hairy like those of the hairy hunter. "Are you really *Esav?"* he asked. For the first time in a long while Isaac wished his vision was not so sorely clouded.

"I am," Jacob replied as confidently as he could muster.

Assured by his son's urging and the rumblings in his stomach, Isaac said, "My son, bring me what you have made.

Sit, indulge your old father with your presence as I eat. My feeble body has worked up an appetite for some wild game. You have brought food to my belly and joy to my soul. Let me now eat so that I may give you my blessing."

Jacob brought the momentous meal to his father. "Here, *abba*, I've brought you some bread and wine to go with it as well."

Isaac ate with relish, satisfied that his firstborn stood before him. It did his declining heart good to think that at last the task that had so long been on his mind would soon be accomplished.

Jacob watched with surprising sadness as his father ate slowly, the woes of aging playing out before his very eyes. The guilt of the deceit weighed like a millstone tied around his neck.

"Come here, my son, and kiss me." Isaac's voice shook Jacob out of his melancholy.

He went to his father and kissed him. When Isaac caught the smell of his clothes, he shuddered with tremulous pleasure.

"Ah, the smell of my son is like the smell of a field that Adonai has blessed. So may God give you dew from heaven, the richness of the earth, and grain and wine in abundance. May peoples serve you and nations bow down to you. May you be lord over your kinsmen, let your mother's descendants bow down to you. Cursed be everyone who curses you, and blessed be everyone who blesses you!"

Father and son breathed a sigh of relief, reveling in pleasure at the long-awaited patriarchal invocation. Tears streamed down both their faces. The Covenant blessing passed on to the next generation. At last. Neither for a moment did each think he was attempting to circumvent *Yahweh's* word or purpose.

"Thank you, *abba*. I will carry your name with honor and reverence and I swear to continue the legacy of your beloved *abba* Abram."

Jacob kissed his father.

Mission accomplished! Walking out of Isaac's tent, elation, triumph and joy intermingled. A conflation of emotions exploded in his soul. He did what he had set out to do. Contended for it. And won. Obtained what he had sought after his entire life. The privileges his brother had disdained, expediently exchanged. For a bowl of stew. Now the prized family blessing was finally his too. Passed down from father to son to son. Abraham, Isaac, and now Jacob. The magnitude and the sheer reality of it washed over his being. Overwhelmed, Jacob paused in front of his tent and wept. Uncontrolled heavings released. Like sudden steam bursting from a pressure valve.

That was where Rebekah found her son. On the ground. Keeled over with undiscerning mourns. Fear seized her heart. Had things gone awry? She half-dragged the man-child inside away from prying eyes.

"Ya'akov, what happened? Tell me, son! Did your father see through your guise? Has his blurry eyes betrayed us after all? Speak to me, Ya'akov!" Rebekah beseeched him.

"No, my mother. *Abba* blessed me. He has blessed me with the blessing of the firstborn!!" Jacob blurted out, his words hanging in gossamer disbelief.

"Oh, Praise! Praise be *Adonai!*" Rebekah's knees slid from beneath her in thankfulness. She had done it. Secured the hallowed benediction for Ya'akov. The younger will no longer be subservient. The older will serve his brother. For the next few moments mother and son sat in silence. Contemplating the insanity of it all. The enormity of their deceit. Their audacious plan so swiftly corroborated, a success.

Till a rancorous bestial roar tore through the air outside.

Twelve

ESAU

Jacob had scarcely left his father's presence when his brother Esau came in from hunting. He had his servant prepare the young ibex he'd hunted and brought it to his father. Then Esau said to Isaac, "My father, please sit up and enjoy your favorite meat, before you give me your blessing."

Isaac asked, "Who are you?"

"Why, *abba*, I am your son," he answered, "your firstborn, *Esav*. Did you forget that you sent me to hunt game for you earlier today? See, I have done what you desire."

Isaac trembled uncontrollably and said, "Then who was it that just brought me the game meal? I ate it all just before you came, and I gave my blessing to him."

When Esau heard his father's words, he burst out with a loud and bitter cry. Immediately both men realized the truth of what had happened. Esau slumped to the ground.

"Bless me—me too, my father!" Esau begged.

But Isaac said, "Your brother ... *Ya'akov* came and took your blessing! Deceitfully!"

With that realization, the bewildered old man sank back into his pillows. Rebekah. The ploy smelled every bit of her touch. Mother and son had tricked him. Their very audacity, an affront to his authority.

"*Ya'akov*! My brother has finally lived up to his name." Esau's voice bellowed in disbelief. "He has supplanted me. Twice—purchased my birthright by cunning, and here, now, now he has stolen my blessing! Usurped my rightful position!" Then he asked his father again, "Haven't you a blessing saved for me, *abba*?"

Isaac answered Esau, "I have made him lord over you and have made all his relatives his servants, and I have sustained him with grain and new wine. The blessing is unalterable. It has *Yahweh's* sanction. That's the unavoidable truth! So what can I possibly do for you, my son?"

"Have you only one blessing, my father? Father, bless me too!" Esau pleaded piteously, weeping aloud.

A sorrowful Isaac answered his pitiable son, "Your dwelling will be away from the earth's richness, my son, away from the dew of heaven above. You will live by the sword and you will serve your brother. But when you break loose, you will shake his yoke off your neck."

Blessing lost. Forever. In its place, a curse—to a dwelling far removed from the luxuries he had always assumed were his. Luxuries of freedom to roam and hunt in the bounty of his childhood land. To be waited on hand and foot by his father's servants. To be applauded and admired by his friends. To be lauded by one and all for his hunting prowess. To succeed Isaac as leader of their tribe. All his entitlements stripped away. Unexpectedly. All while he was away at their father's request, hunting for game. Life's cruel irony.

"Serve my brother? Never!" A virulent grievous growl inflamed with hate, bitterness and vengeance emitted till he was almost breathless with anguish.

Unrepentant, Esau had not cried, *"Abba,* I have done wrong. This is just punishment on me for having so readily exchanged my birthright to assuage my hunger." No, Esau's tears were only for himself. His naivete in assuming that his twin had not the wiles nor the guts to defraud him, first in plain sight and now by beating him to the chase infuriated him. He hated himself for his own dereliction. Hated his father for his frailty. Isaac's blindness had led him to innocently give away Esau's blessing to Jacob. Hated his mother for her complicity. Of this he had no doubt. Rebekah was behind the dupery. Esau hated his twin brother for the latter's swindling. Swearing revenge he declared, "The time for mourning my father will soon come, and then I will kill Jacob."

Thirteen

REBEKAH & ISAAC

Hearing this deadly vow from Esau's two wives, Rebekah's heart swung like a pendulum. Between fear and resolve. She must warn Jacob of Esau's intent. Convince Isaac to separate their sons. Three. Three men in her life. She was about to lose one to sorrow. Another to wrath-filled vengeance. To lose the third, and her favorite, to his brother's malevolence would be the end of her. No, Rebekah refused to cave in to fear. She had to act. Again. Immediately. Beg, cajole, persuade. Whatever it would take to keep the fast-crumbling peace in the family. Rebekah hurried to her husband's side.

"*Rivkah,* is that you?" Isaac asked as soon as Rebekah entered. As dim sighted as his eyes had deteriorated to, Isaac was always able to still pick out his wife's footfalls no matter how quietly she tried to tiptoe around him.

"Yes, *Yitz'chak,* it is I," Rebekah sighed

"What have you done, *Rivkah?* Does not the lament of your firstborn rip your soul as it does mine? How could you resort to such trickery? Such a debasing of my authority? How could you?" Tears of disbelief coursed down Isaac's wrinkled face. All of his 137 years of living pitiably sapped out from his broken heart.

"How could I, you ask, *Yitz'chak?*" Rebekah threw back her husband's question. "How could *you* conspire with *Esav* to bestow the blessing in my absence. *Our* absence? Are we not a family too, *Ya'akov* and I? Is not the blessing a traditional communal celebration, to be bestowed in the presence of *Adonai?* Why the secrecy, my husband? Why?"

Isaac was at once stunned and shamed by his wife's retort. Silence, taut and frayed, filled the air. Prophecy's fulfillment was not theirs after all to attain. *Yahweh* was sovereign, His will not to be thwarted. Ever. This humbling realization triggered another bout of violent trembling in Isaac. Husband and wife slumped beside each other. Their simultaneous betrayals laid bare between them. A chasm so deep and sharp seared through their once impenetrable love. Distrust, fear, lies, falsehood now rent the marital relationship. How had they come to this? At this late stage. When they were supposed to enjoy the rest of their golden years. How could Isaac now leave this world in peace? Sorrow drenched their hearts, their minds numbed by the abysmal realization of their individual misdeeds.

But the very thought of murder tearing asunder the family once the patriarch was gone from this earth shook Rebekah out of her regret. With Isaac gone she knew that she and Jacob would be at Esau's mercy. It would be too late then.

"*Esav* has sworn to kill *Ya'akov* once you have joined your ancestors, *Yitz'chak!* You must not allow this to happen, my husband. I would not be bereft of my entire family with one blow." Rebekah pleaded with Isaac.

"What would you have us do, *Rivkah?*" a depleted Isaac asked. "What can this feeble body do to undo the chaos we have all created?" he continued helplessly.

"It is *Esav's* heathen wives that have turned his heart away from *Yahweh*. Their constant sneering at our ways has turned our firstborn to belittle his birthright and despise all things spiritual until it has come to this. I hate the Hittite women! One son led astray is more than we can both bear. If *Ya'akov* also marries a Hittite woman, like those who live here, my life won't be worth living." she declared.

Isaac's aggrieved soul had lost all spirit. Let the family do what their hearts tell them. Wearied beyond measure, he did not argue with his wife's plea.

Jacob too had heard his brother's bestial roar, had anticipated his murderous retaliation. Now their mother stood before him confirming both. What had he done? His brother's bones burned with vengeance. Their father's brittle frame threatened to disintegrate with grief. What had they done, mother and son? How had their once relatively harmonious family so swiftly become a cauldron of poisonous brew? His heart lurched in a torrent of regret and shame. Remorse for the anguish his secret scheme had brought upon his parents. Shame for his coveting that which was not his.

'*Ya'akov*, are you listening to me?" his mother's voice broke through Jacob's turmoil.

"*Esav* is comforting himself by planning to kill you. My son, listen to me. Get up and go to Laban, my brother in

Haran. Stay with him a little while, until your brother's anger subsides. Your brother's anger will turn away from you, and he will forget what you did to him. Then I'll send for your safe return. Why should I lose both sons on the same day?"

So Jacob was summoned to his parent's tent. Ashen, he stood before his despondent *abba*. The father whose love he had hungered for his whole life. The man whose approval meant everything to Jacob. The leader whose mantle he had fastidiously sought to assume. The aged elder whose piercing blind eyes Jacob's own were now too guilty to meet. For an eternity father and son beheld each other's broken countenance. For an eternity each bore the other's sorrow, shamed by their personal secret covetousness gone askance. Silence hung a stranglehold for an eternity around their necks.

Then in a voice quivering with emotion, Isaac charged his younger son, "You are not to choose a wife from among the Hittite women. Go now to the home of *B'tu'el* your mother's father, and choose a wife there from the daughters of Laban, your mother's brother. May *El Shaddai* bless you, make you fruitful and increase your descendants until they become a whole assembly of peoples. And may he give you the blessing which he gave Abraham, you and your descendants with you, so that you will possess the land you will travel through, the land God gave to Abraham."

His mother's decision earlier divulged to him in quiet now spoke into existence. Jacob wept as the words wavered from his father's quivering lips. Discordant words of banishment interspersed with a spiritual blessing. What an irony. He bravely stepped to the elder's feeble form and clasped his beloved *abba* to his bosom.

The hurried farewell was as heart-wrenching as it was furtive. Jacob, amazed by Rebekah's strength of character in the midst of the catastrophe, acquiesced to her every command. He prayed this parting would be only temporary as she was adamant it would be. Till Esau's outrage had burnt to a cinder, his damaged ego soothed by distractions. Neither mother nor son knew how long that would take. Rebekah prayed for Jacob's safe journey. The exile, a necessary evil. Time was of the essence. There was no telling how long the false peace between the brothers would last. She busied her hands with filling her precious son's camel with the essentials for the trek to Paddan-Aram. Not till he was out of his brother's reach would she breathe freely.

Mother and son bade a stoic farewell. Grief-laden that their gambit had come to this. That it had impetuously exploded in their faces so abruptly. Their celebration cruelly turned disastrous. With grave remorse Jacob left the beloved mother who had stood by him his entire life. Wordlessly Rebekah stared into the horizon, her son's slumped shoulders diminishing into a specter before he disappeared altogether. Her silent prayers wafted with him in petition and hope. Hope in the promise whispered to her heart at the birth of her warring twins. Hope—the strand she clung tenaciously to.

Fourteen

ESAU

Word soon got to Esau that Jacob had left. If nothing else, his wives had their ears to the grapevine like bees to honey. Adah, daughter of Elon, the Hittite knew that nothing pleased her husband more than the latest village trifle against his twin. And Oholibamah, daughter of Anah, the Hivite was ever eager to add her own tidbit. So, the conniver had slipped through his grasp after all! Not waiting till their father was dead and gone but sent off by Isaac himself with the old man's blessings. The knife wound drove deeper and more hurtful into Esau's heart.

"Did you know that your father had strictly commanded your brother with these words, 'Do NOT marry a Canaanite woman'?" Adah had spat out the words to her husband. "What are we? Chaff? Worthless husks? Broken straw to be blown away by the wind? These can only be the words of Rebekah. Your mother!" she added.

"And Jacob had obeyed, like the dumb sheep you always said your brother was. Sent to your mother's family in

Paddan Aram, to find a 'suitable' wife." Oholibamah chimed after Adah.

Esau's irritation with his wives grew with their every haughty word. For he now realized how displeasing his Canaanite women were to his parents. They had not dared to openly criticize his wives when he had brought first Adah, then Oholibamah home. Though the look his mother gave them both bespoke her mind. But Esau hardly had regard for what Rebekah thought anyway. It was his father's opinion that counted. And in Isaac's eyes, his firstborn could do no wrong. Or so Esau had always thought. Till now.

Esau was determined to right the wrong he had inflicted upon his beloved *abba*. On the quiet one day he rode alone into the desert. No one knew where he was headed. Not Adah, not Oholibamah. Not any of his hunting friends. Esau was gone for two whole months.

Rebekah and Isaac were thankful for his absence. Perhaps the journey would be his soothing balm and simmer down his rage against his brother. Peace settled in the household. Till one blistering day when the sun was at its zenith Esau's camel came into view. He was not alone. With him was another figure. Curious eyes greeted them when they drew near.

"Abba, imma', meet Mahalath, my new bride. She is the sister of Nebaioth." Esau turned to look at Isaac. Hopeful for a hint of recognition in the elder's mind. When none surfaced, he added, "She is the daughter of your brother, Ishmael, *abba.*"

The sound of his estranged brother's name jolted Isaac from his confusion.

"*Yishma'el?* You went looking for a wife from my father *Abram's* family?" Isaac queried in amazement.

"Yes, *abba!* This is cousin Mahalath," Esau reiterated, his eyes not leaving his father's face.

Rebekah stared at her latest daughter-in-law, her heart toward Esau softening. Perhaps his wrath against his brother had subsided. Perhaps it was time for her too to trust her firstborn now. Perhaps his remorse for devaluing things that mattered to his parents changed him. Perhaps now with her younger son gone she could rightly love his twin.

As Esau and Mahalath stood hopeful and shy before his parents, a flood of memories threatened to undo Rebekah. Memories of a time long, long ago. A time from before she and Isaac had any children. A time from before Esau and Jacob were conceived. A time when love alone did not produce babies.

Love alone most certainly did not produce the son that Rebekah and Isaac pined for. Days had turned into months. Months into years.

"Twenty-five years to fulfill a promise," Rebekah remembered Isaac telling her about his own birth. Who could blame his mother, Sarah, for taking things into her own hands after patient years of nothing? Nagging and needling, Sarah had urged her husband to sleep with her Egyptian handmaid in the hope of a son to present her beloved Abraham. Rebekah could see herself acquiescing to the same resort. It was customary. In fact, expected, even where her parents lived. "Perhaps I should suggest it to Isaac myself," she mused. "After all, we have ourselves been married for twenty years." Yearning replaced hope.

O, how Rebekah's own heart had ached with the barrenness of her womb, her infertility an agonizing affront each time she beheld a friend's newborn. A shame that the beautiful body her beloved pleasured in could bear no offspring, carry no man-seed. Each time she'd held Isaac to her breast after their coming together—he, spent with release, and she yielded to their passion—an anguished yearning to be with child inevitably would become her wordless prayer. Why won't *Yahweh* hear her? "*Adonai* forbid that I, like my husband's mother, bear seed only in my dotage!" Rebekah silently cried out in distress. "Are you not the One who is said to heal the brokenhearted and bind wounds? The One who names and numbers the stars? O crush not my weakened spirit!"

Desperation seeped into her pores. Led her to stealthily seek the help of Adama, the spiritist. Only when Isaac was away on business, mind you. He would have disapproved had he known. Heartened her instead to not despair and smothered her with his kisses and assurances of patience and trust in *Yahweh* instead. She remembered the idols Bethuel kept in the corner of her parent's tent. Tonight she would light incense to the one idol she had secretly hidden away.

But Adama was vague. "Daughter, I sense a disquiet in you. But I see nothing else at this time. Come back when you are in a better mood." Rebekah slunk out of the old woman's tent in disappointment. Yet again.

Laying in the arms of her beloved husband that night, Rebekah gently broached the subject.

"*Yitz'chak*, my love, perhaps you should take Alysha into your tent. Perhaps like what your mother did for your father Abraham with her hand-maid, Hagar, that could then bring about a miracle for us too?" Rebekah whispered to her husband.

"Rebekah, Rebekah, *Adonai* forbid it that we dare test Him this way!" Isaac recoiled. Instantly. "Have you not heard where THAT led to?! Have you forgotten about my abandoned brother, Ishmael?"

Isaac then pulled Rebekah to his chest. "Let me tell you a secret. The secret of how my *abba* got his name. Did you know that grandfather Terah had three sons?"

"What good does three sons of grandfather Terah have to do with us, Isaac, when we have NONE ourselves?" Rebekah demanded with irritation.

"Shhh—Shhh, my beautiful wife. Listen, and you will understand. Of the three sons of grandfather Terah, my *abba* was named *'Abram'*—'the father is exalted.' That was *abba's* name for almost half of his life. A good strong name, *'Abram',* don't you agree?"

"Get to the point, Isaac, unless you want to sleep alone tonight," his impatient wife warned.

"Why such impatience, Rebekah. A good story needs time in the telling. This one is especially good. And worth every minute in its recount." Isaac loved teasing her. "*Abba* Abraham was *abba Abram* until one fateful day. In his ninety-ninth year, when *imma Sarai* … did you know that was my mother's birth name?" Isaac turned to ask Rebekah.

"I may have heard it in passing but never paid much attention to it." she answered. "But you were telling me about your father's name, not your *imma's*" she reminded her long-winded husband.

"Ah, yes, my dearest *abba*, bless his memory! One day, in his ripe age of ninety-nine, *Adonai* appeared to him. I can only imagine what that encounter must have been like. *Adonai* came to *abba Abram* and said, *"I am El Shaddai, the All-Sufficient One. Walk in my presence and be pure-hearted. I will make my covenant between me and you, and I will increase your numbers greatly."*

Abba Abram fell on his face in fear! But the Mighty One continued speaking with him: *"As for me, this is my covenant with you: you will be the father of many nations. Your name will no longer be Abram. From this moment forward your name will be Abraham—Father of Many—because I have made you the father of many nations. I will cause you to be very fruitful. I will make nations of you, kings will descend from you."*

It was incomprehensible. *Abba* lay there on the ground, prostrate. Still as stone. But *Adonai* was not done. He continued by saying these strange words, *"I am establishing my covenant between me and you, along with your descendants after you, generation after generation, as an everlasting covenant, to be God for you and for your descendants after you. I will give you and your descendants after you the land in which you are now foreigners, all the land of Kena'an, as a permanent possession; and I will be their God."*

"It was a holy moment, Rebekah. A moment like no other. *Abba's* defining moment. Because long after that encounter, *imma* became with child. It was a miracle. *I* was that child, Rebekah. Conceived out of a sacred covenant." Isaac's voice spoke in awe. "A covenant of descendants, generation after generation, Rebekah. Think upon it, my beloved. We will have children, you and I."

Isaac's faith had been contagious. For at once, Rebekah pleaded, "Then speak to *Adonai*, my husband. Ask for the promised child. I do not need more. Just one. One is all I ask. One from your own loins and mine."

"Indeed, I will. Come. Together we will seek *Yahweh*, you and I, together." Isaac had readily agreed.

"*O, El Shaddai*, Mighty One, we humbly come before you at this moment. As you covenanted with my *abba*, changing his name to *Abraham*, Father of Many Nations, we ask that that may come true. From our very own bodies. We beseech you for the blessing of a child so that the covenant of descendants, generation after generation, may come to pass."

The strength of her husband's prayer quieted Rebekah's spirit that propitious night. In holy peace they slept afterward. Amazingly, not long after Rebekah became pregnant. The Lord had answered Isaac's prayer and more. For not one, but two sons, were given them. At once, twins.

And the older one now stood before them. With a new wife. A woman from Abraham's own loins. Daughter of Abraham's son, Ishmael, brother of Isaac. *Adonai* Yir'eh— *Adonai* will see to it—had once again provided. He had seen to it that Jacob would be safely away from his angered brother, and that Esau would return seeking peace with his parents. All four embraced. A wedding party would be their comfort.

The wedding was a joyous festive occasion. A celebration that had not been had in a very long time in their household. Marred only by the absence of Jacob. But this was Esau's day. His and Mahalath's, Isaac and Rebekah reminded themselves.

They were determined that once more the sounds of joy and gladness, the voices of bride and groom would surround them. The faction between their sons had come to a head. Jacob had to leave unexpectedly and most reluctantly. Esau then left as well, unexpectedly, but voluntarily. Stormed out hurt, vindictive, unforgiving. Without a word if he would ever return. But he did. Return willingly. With a bride in tow. And not just any bride. Not another woman from a pagan tribe. But a relative. A descendant of *abba* Abraham himself. Seeing no need for a matchmaker, he had made for himself a good marital match at last, with his first cousin. It was an alliance that Isaac had always longed and hoped for but not expected to happen in this late stage.

No expense was thus too much for the wedding celebration. Under the wedding canopy, a beaming Esau stood with shy Mahalath. With wine in his shaking hand, old Isaac's voice trembled as he pronounced the blessing after the couple had finalized their vows. A blessing for love and harmony, peace and companionship upon their new life together. Father and son eyed each other. Hope, happiness, forgiveness writ large upon their faces. Rebekah could not help but feel relieved that her husband's recent sorrow was forgotten. For now at least. Noise and fanfare flowed freely with wine and food. A feast like no other, celebrating marriage, new life, forgiveness, restoration and reconciliation. Family heartaches and disappointments, hard lessons caused by lies, manipulations, and schemes will hopefully be things of the past.

A week after the celebrations, Esau paid a personal visit to his parents. A lightness of heart visible in his eagerness to speak with them both. His father was especially glad to see his firstborn at peace again.

"*Esav*, my son, come sit with us. We have been waiting to hear your story. How did you meet Mahalath? Where did you know to find her? How is my brother, *Yishma'el?*" So many questions rolled unheeded from the happy old man's lips.

"*Shalom, abba. Shalom, imma.* It is good to be home. A joy that I have not ever before felt has befallen upon me, thanks be to *Adonai.*" Esau replied as he sat himself beside Isaac and Rebekah.

"As you know, my hurt was deep and my outrage dark when Jacob had stolen what was mine. I vowed to myself that death would be his penalty. But not when you're still with us, *abba.* After. After you're gone. I would bide my time. Drink and women would drown my wrath. That was my plan." Esau began his surprising confession.

"My heart was anguished within me that Jacob, my very own brother, would deceive me and so cunningly at that! But when I saw him leave, shoulders slumbered in shocked disbelief and misery, sent away by you, something wrenched inside of me. In getting what he had now obviously yearned for for a long time in secret he had lost his family in the process. I had never expected that to happen, *abba, imma.* Believe me when I tell you this. I have never wanted our family to be torn apart this way. Ever." Rebekah sat up straighter on hearing her son's declaration. She had mistaken his brazen behavior. He was not heartless after all. He cared after all for family.

Esau gave a knowing nod to his mother. "Yes, I had never shown any care for what mattered to Jacob. I cared only for what gave me pleasure and fun. Rights and blessings had always been mine to be had. Never a doubt crossed my mind that they could ever be taken away, *abba*. Not till it was stolen from me did I realize their meaning. Their purpose. And when that happened, it was my pride that had been hurt. I am ashamed to admit that. I was a fool. Standoffish. Boastful. An ungrown man." He continued.

"When word got to my ears that you had sent Jacob away for his own safety, from me, his twin, I was shamefaced. Then you made him swear that he will not take a foreign woman for a wife. And he promised. That he would do as you desire made me realize that I had always done as I desired. Not what would please you, my beloved parents. Only what would please me. Jacob is more worthy of your love. I now recognize that. That night that he left, I made it my goal to right the wrong that I had so carelessly done to you."

Never in their lifetime did Isaac and Rebekah think to ever hear such words come from the mouth of Esau. Stunned, they sat, the profoundness of it all washing a torrent over their souls. The stranger that had ridden away in rage now returned. A changed man. Unceasing wonders.

"You remember old Deena, my nurse-maid? She had sometimes spoken of Hagar and Ishmael. I had always been curious about your brother, *abba*. The uncle I remind you of. A wild donkey of a man but also the most avid archer was what *abba Abraham* described to you. Deena told me where I might find them." Esau told his parents.

"How is *Yishma'el?*" Isaac asked eagerly.

"Hagar said uncle Ishmael joined his ancestors fourteen years ago. I am sorry to tell you this, *abba*. But they had twelve sons and Mahalath is one of their two daughters. I have fourteen cousins!!" Esau's excitement at this discovery mirrored the delight on his father's face.

"What a welcome I was received with in their home in Egypt, *imma*. I will never forget their warm hospitality." he continued.

At the mention of Hagar's name, Rebekah blushed with guilt at the remembrance of her own unwelcoming of her first two daughters-in-law. "And how is Hagar, *Esav?*" Rebekah asked.

"Hagar is getting on in age. But a proud and happy grandmother with her many grandchildren. She pulled me aside one day and said returning to Egypt was the best thing that had happened to her and Ishmael. Not at first. Cast out into the desert by the man who fathered her child was beyond her imagination. For many years she had held on to much bitterness toward him and Sarah as you can expect. But she told me this strangest encounter of her wilderness abandonment with teenage Ishmael." Esau went on to recount Hagar's story.

Fifteen

HAGAR

The evening's heated conversation with Sarah had ended in an impasse. Before storming into the shadow of night, she had issued her bewildered husband an ultimatum. Inaction on his part would cause a war between the two women and their sons. In a single swift swoop, he stood to lose everyone that mattered most to him. Contorted in a tangled web of distress, guilt and dilemma, Abraham roused his weary bones from bed. Sleep had eluded him on this joyous occasion—the weaning of baby Isaac. What lay ahead was a necessary but grievous task. *Adonai* had bid him do as Sarah had asked. But this did nothing to ease the repugnance of it all. Darkness pervaded his soul. Abraham rued the day he had given in to his wife's urgings and impregnated her handmaid.

Hagar was shaken out of her sleep by Abraham's entrance into the tent she shared with their son, Ishmael. In his hands were three loaves of bread and a skin of water. "Freshly baked," he'd said sheepishly. "By Deena," he quickly added.

Wiping the sleep from her eyes, Hagar could not help noticing how those strong hands of her master were shaking as he held out the offerings. For that's what they were. His sorry offerings for what was about to happen. Hagar knew something was amiss when Sarah had shoved her aside during the preparations for Isaac's weaning ceremony with her warning, "Be careful, Hagar, Ishmael will not mock his brother without consequences." But she had never expected this indignation. Cast out a second time. She had thought that the gift of Ishmael was the guarantee of a safe permanent home for them both. For wasn't that what *Adonai* had meant when the All-Seeing One had instructed her to return and submit to her mistress when she had run away the first time? He had assured that her descendants would be too numerous to count. Had she misconstrued those sacred words?

By then Ishmael too had awakened. Abraham pulled his bewildered son to his breast in a tight rigid hug, the look on his wrinkled face an agonizing misery.

"*Yishma'el,* my son. Look after your mother. You cannot stay here any longer. May *Adonai* watch over you both in your journey. Go back with her to your Egyptian family. They will be happy to meet their grandson. You and your mother will have a better life there," Abraham spoke in an almost hushed whisper. The words were an enigma to the teenager's ears.

Tearing himself abruptly out this sudden embrace, Abraham averted his eyes from Ishmael's shocked face. Comprehension of the situation was creeping over the boy as he took in his father's words and brusque actions. Before either mother and son had a chance to recover from their rude awakening, Abraham had put the leathern goatskin bottle on Hagar's shoulders, shoved the bread loaves in Ishmael's hands and slunk out of the tent, his sandals clacking like harsh slaps on their faces.

They were being sent away. For good this time. In no uncertain terms. No room for negotiation whatsoever. Deena, who had been eavesdropping outside, slid right in after master Abraham had made his hasty retreat. Tears crinkled down the old nursemaid's face as she briskly helped Hagar and Ishmael pack.

"Be quick, my boy, before the rest awake. Less seen fewer explanations needed. The gods go with you. You are strong and young. I have put some goat cheese and yogurt in this bag. That should sustain you both for the next few days." Deena plunked a cloth-filled bag onto Ishmael's donkey before turning to Hagar.

The younger servant stood speechless before her only true friend. "In time you will come into your own, Hagar. Of this I am sure. For did you not tell me of what the Great One had spoken to you before your son was born? Your descendants will be innumerable just like He said. Hold on to that promise, Hagar. Tightly. Never let it go. Remind Him when you begin to despair. It is good to remind Him that this son of yours is also the seed of master Abraham."

With those words ringing in her ears, Hagar sat on the ass as her son led them both away from the only home Ishmael had ever known. For days they wandered in the desert around Be'er-Sheva, living on the provisions swiftly shoved into their hands that fateful morning. No other soul journeyed with them. It was as if the earth had banished everyone else from their presence. Ishmael's stoic silence terrified his mother. By day they walked wordlessly, each one deep in their own thoughts. By night, they slept in caves and makeshift shelters. The bitter reality of their predicament sinking deeper with each day's grating journey.

One night when the water was gone, Hagar left her son sleeping under a bush. She went a bow-shot's distance away and sat down on a rock. The moonless night's darkness overwhelmed her ragged soul as she wept. "Where are you, *El Roi?* Do you not see me as you once saw me? Look at us now! How long will you forget me? How long must you hide your face from me?" Hagar cried out.

"Let me die if you must. But not Ishmael. You said to name him Ishmael. So I did. I listened to you because I heard you. Or so I thought. You promised me that my descendants would be many. Numberless you said. Look at us now. Look at us! Do we look like anything but dust to you? I can't bear to watch my child die. Just let me die before he does."

Awakened by his mother's lament, Ishmael watched her wail into the night's nothingness. The unbearable sight seared into his spirit and he let out a gasp of despair. *Adonai* heard the boy's anguish.

Then a voice, tender and strong, spoke into Hagar's devastation.

"Don't be afraid, Hagar. Adonai never forgets His word. What's wrong with you that you have forgotten who He is? Because He has heard the voice of the boy in his present situation, you will be alone no more. Get up, lift Ishmael up, and hold him tightly in your hand, because I am going to make him a

great nation." With these words, both Hagar and Ishmael fell into a deep sleep.

The next morning when Hagar opened her eyes, she saw a well of water in the not too far distance. Wiping the sleep from her eyes, she dragged her body back to where Ishmael was sleeping. "Ishmael, Ishmael, wake up! Wake up, son!" she shook the lad as hard as she could.

Dried blood had crusted on Ishmael's cracked lips. "I am sorry, mother. There is nothing left to eat or drink. I am no longer the son who can look after his poor mother. I am not the son of the great Abraham. I have let my father and you down. Just let me sleep and die here."

Ishmael's death wish shook Hagar out of her own despair. With whatever little strength left in her emaciated body she fixed her eyes on the mirage ahead and dragged her bedraggled self forward. When she arrived at the well, tears of relief blinded her eyes. It was no mirage. The well stood in the barren desert. And no one was about. Not a soul. Just the hope-filled well and her. Lowering the bucket tied to the end of the rope, Hagar heaved the weight up and drank straight from the bucket. The water cascaded over her parched throat. No longer would she, Hagar, ever waste a drop of water in her life thereafter. Ever. With that silent vow, she then filled the skin and returned to her despondent child. Lifting his head up in one hand, she gave Ishmael the water to drink.

"And that was how we survived, Esau," Hagar ended her story to Abraham's grandson.

"*Adonai* was with us the rest of the way till we got to Egypt. Ishmael grew and grew as I never thought he would.

The bitterness of our exile slowly seeped away from our souls. I found him a wife here in Egypt. But he could never leave the desert. That sojourn hardened his resolve to live and show his father who had let him go that he was a survivor. Ishmael chose the Pa'ran Desert for his home. He has done well. As you can see, I am content. Had we continued to live with your grandparents, Esau, we would always have been foreigners. Slaves for life. So, in hindsight, Sarah did us a great favor to send us away. Be sure to tell your *abba* I said so, Esau. Isaac must not carry his parent's guilt nor live in regret into his last years."

Not a dry eye was left as Esau shared Hagar and Ishmael's story with his stunned parents.

Sixteen

JACOB

Beersheba. The place of oath and covenant and completion. Where Abraham had first dug and claimed a well and signed a treaty with Abimelek. Where seven ewe lambs were used to seal that treaty. The "Well of Seven" as it was sometimes known. The place where years later Isaac had unearthed and reopened his *abba's* wells. And water flowed, fresh and free, and peace and harvest and wealth were testaments of *Adonai's* blessings.

The place where Jacob and Esau had spent childhood hours playing under *abba* Abraham's tamarisk tree. The tree under which *abba Abraham* himself had called on *Adonai* for many years, which Jacob had sought and secretly claimed as his own sacred space. Beersheba was home. Jacob's home. His first. His best. His solid ground. And now he had to leave, broken. Broken dreams. Broken family. Broken heart. Broken spirit. Broken life. All because in his profound desire after his *abba's* holy blessing he had inadvertently taken the path of fool's wisdom. How could he and his mother have been so wrong? They had both believed *Adonai's* promise and were so sure that the blessing was his to inherit, not Esau's.

It was a broken man who lurched forward on his camel that fateful day. Each sway, each slow rocking motion fissured, a dull ugly splintering of his broken heart. Regret, a useless deplorable grief, haunted his every thought. What lay ahead he could not foresee. Paddan Aram, a land at once blurry and unfamiliar across the river Euphrates. Grandfather Bethuel and uncle Laban he knew only as names. An unknown stranger woman to take as a wife of his own. What did he know of marriage except for stolen glances and secret stirrings? How will he begin to sew the gossamer threads of his life without even a skein of hope? When will he see his parents again? If ever. Jacob could not bear to look back at Beersheba lest it be a curse.

Solitude could not be a better companion in times of doubt and confusion. The events of Jacob's life played out like a map in his mind as he trekked alone. No twin to contend with, no father to please nor mother to side with him. Nothing was astir save the padding of his camel's plods and the tumult of his thoughts. The sounds of silence reverberated with the heat of the burning sand. Its wilderness, stark, barren, elemental, was deep calling to deep. All the time in the world to think with no one and nothing to muck up his brain. His years of manipulation and games had finally caught up with him. Shame and guilt conspired to condemn him.

At day's end a darkening hue of dense ebony began to fill the sky. Soon it would not be safe to travel alone. Jacob decided to stop for the night as the sun bid its gradual farewell. He was grateful for the cool evening. Too tired to think of food, he chewed on a handful of dried dates and a piece of flatbread his mother had bundled for him, washing it down with sips of wine from the old wineskin. Then he laid his head on a stone and stared into the brittle black. Tears of sorrow, despair, alienation and loneliness flowed unbidden. No one was about. Estranged from his family. Estranged from all that he loved. Estranged from his true self. Estranged from the God of his fathers. Lying in the darkness on the hard desert ground in his solitude in the valley of his despair no one was around to see his stricken tears as the events of the past played over and over in his mind. Wearied in body, mind and spirit, Jacob did not know when sleep came upon him. Because...

Heaven suddenly opened up. That much Jacob knew. He had never seen heaven before. But somehow he knew what lay before his eyes was heaven. Where black clouds and deep darkness surrounded him when he laid his head to rest, now blazing light, without sun or moon, spanned the vistas. Amazingly his eyes were able to take in the unspeakable brilliance. He saw. O, did he ever see! A ladder hung in the air. From heaven it touched the earth's ground. Angels in bright raiment descended and ascended the luminous steps of that magnificent ladder. Spellbound, Jacob knew he wanted to ascend with the angels. To go up to heaven with them. To be with them in his lonely estrangement. But before he could rouse himself to take his first step, suddenly *Adonai* stood beside him. Beside him, Jacob, the manipulator, the one who had estranged himself by his supplanting of his own twin brother, by his deception of his own father. *Adonai* stood beside Jacob. And the look in the Holy One's eyes. Jacob could not look back into those seeing eyes that saw into his soul. For they were not eyes of condemnation. Love and understanding and compassion instead filled the look. Then *Adonai* spoke.

"I am Adonai, the God of your abbas, Abram and Yit'zhak. The land on which you are lying I will give to you and to your descendants. Your descendants will be as numerous as the grains of dust on the earth. You will expand to the west and to the east, to the north and to the south. By you and your descendants all the families of the earth will be blessed. Look, I will be with you. I will guard you wherever you go, and I will bring you back into this land, because I won't leave you until I have done what I have promised you."

At the bottom of that heavenly ladder, *Adonai* stood beside Jacob. The irrationality of it all shook Jacob awake, his dream as vivid as the sun's arc peeking over the new day.

"Surely, *Adonai* is in this place—and I didn't know it!"

His face was drenched. Not with rain nor with the morning dew. But with the heaving sobs of disbelief and relief when he heard those four simple words—*'I am with you'*—spoken by *Adonai* to him.

Four simple words.

He had sought to climb the stairs to heaven but heaven's Creator himself had sought him out. Came. Stood alongside him. There in the desert wilderness. Spoke life-giving words. Of companionship in his loneliness. Of forgiveness in his guilt-ridden sorrow. Of love in the affirmation with his relationships with his fathers, Abraham and Isaac. Of fulfillment in his covenant blessing of land and descendants of his very own. Of protection in his sojourn into the unknown. Of return and hopeful reconciliation with his family. Of covenant. Of divine Presence.

Where once tears of sorrow, regret and remorse coursed his heart, *Adonai's* voice purified, changing everything. Jacob had no language to describe it. Safe that the words that were released from that voice washed a soothing balm over Jacob's troubled soul of yesterday. He had heard the voice of the God of his fathers. Encountered the sanctity of that holy presence. For himself. It was inconceivable. It was scarcely dawn.

Then he became afraid.

"This place is fearsome! This has to be the gate of heaven, the house of God!!"

Shuddering from the sacred encounter, he took the stone he had put under his head, and set it up as a standing-stone. He rummaged among his belongings on the camel's back frantically searching for what he needed. Soon his hands felt the roughness of the familiar vial. Drawing it out, his eyes glinted with joy. Careful not to waste a single precious drop, he poured the olive oil on top of the stone, the rock pillow on which he had laid his troubled head the night before and arisen this morning transformed. It would be his personal memorial stone of his first meeting with the unseen One. Not in a million years would he ever forget this holy ground. Jacob named the place *Beit-El,* house of God.

Emboldened by what he had heard and seen in the dream, Jacob took this vow: "If *Adonai* will be with me as I heard him say and will guard me on this road that I am traveling, giving me bread to eat and clothes to wear so that I return to my father's house in peace, then *Adonai* will be *my* God; and this stone, which I have set up as a standing-stone, will be God's house; and of everything given me, I will faithfully return one-tenth to you, *Adonai.*"

Jacob set out that morning, a new man. Restored. Calmed as never before by a mysterious peace, wonder and amazement continued to swim through his thoughts. His heart was ablaze with excitement for what lay ahead. Heading east toward Paddan-Aram a perpetual grin played on his face. His mother would be delighted to hear all that he had to share of his sacred encounter. Thoughts of Rebekah caused him to look at where he was going. Before long he noticed movement. Sheep, four flocks worth, were lying down in an open field. Drawing closer he came upon a well. It was a well, commonly used by shepherds. When all the flocks were gathered, the shepherd would roll the stone from the well and water the sheep. It was a big well covered with a hefty stone slab.

Approaching the shepherds, Jacob said, "Shalom."

"Shalom," they replied, eyeing him with curiosity. But before they could say another word, Jacob spoke first,

"If I may ask, where are you from?"

"We're from Haran," they answered. "Where are you from?"

Hearing that familiar name, Jacob's heart skipped a beat.

"Would you happen to know Laban, grandson of Nahor?"

"We do." The shepherds replied.

"Are things well with him?" Jacob continued.

"Why, very well," they said. "Speaking of Laban, here comes his daughter, Rachel, to water his flock."

Jacob could not believe his good luck! But he pretended not to sound too eager.

"Why are you not watering your flocks so they can get back to grazing? It is only mid-day, not time to herd them home yet, is it?" he queried further.

"No, no, most definitely lots of daylight left. But as you can see, that is one heavy stone cover. We wait for all the shepherds to get here. Together we will be able to roll the stone from the well," they replied.

At that moment, Jacob saw Rachel nearing with her father, Laban's sheep. He quickly nudged his camel down, leapt from the creature's back and headed straight for the well. Without any hesitation, he single-handedly rolled the hulk of a stone from the mouth of the well, leaving Rachel and the other shepherds gaping. Then with a cavalier sweep of his hands, Jacob invited Rachel to the watering hole.

Surprised by the stranger's gesture, Rachel led her flock to him.

"Shalom, kind master," she said, looking directly into his eyes. Then she noticed his tearing up. It was a rare sight to behold in a man so physically strong. But before she could ask more, he came up to her and kissed her in greeting!

"Shalom, Rachel," Jacob muttered. "Pardon my emotion. I am Jacob, son of your father Laban's sister, Rebekah."

Hearing her aunt's name, Rachel's hand leapt to her mouth in shock. "Jacob, you say? Son of Rebekah, you say?

What are you doing here so far from home? Are you by yourself?" All of her astonishment rolled into those questions.

Jacob could not contain himself further. While the sheep were being watered, they sat under the shade of a tree and he told Rachel a bit about his family.

"Wait, don't say another word," Rachel interrupted. "My father needs to hear this." Without further ado, she hitched herself up and ran to tell her father.

"*Abba, abba* Laban. Come quick! You won't believe who I just met," she yelled when she neared home.

"Slow down, my Rachel. Who did you meet? Slow down so I can understand what you're saying."

"Jacob, *abba,* Jacob, he said his name was. Son of your sister, Rebekah!"

When Laban heard his sister's name, he started. "Are you sure you heard right, Rachel? Rebekah, who went away to be married to the son of uncle Abraham?" he asked, doubtfully.

"Yes, Yes, that uncle Abraham. And the man's name is Jacob. Come now, *abba*. You must meet him and hear what he has to tell us himself.

Laban ran with Rachel to meet Jacob. When they got to the well, he saw that his sheep had all been watered. Standing quite breathless before Jacob, Laban stared at the former. There were his sister's unmistakable dimples on both sides of the man's mouth, and her cheeky smile. Laban embraced his nephew with a kiss.

"Come, Come, Jacob. You're my flesh and blood! My family! Come, we must celebrate!" Laban enthused.

Jacob was thrilled. "Wait, uncle Laban. Let me first help these men cover the well before we go."

With those words, the shepherds all rose in one accord and helped Jacob roll the stone over the well. Eager to hear more of the man's story, they followed hopefully behind. But when they got to Laban's, the look on the latter's face told them they would have to hear the story another time. Disappointed, they herded their sheep to their own homes.

Inside the tent, while the women prepared the welcome meal, Jacob told Laban the story of everything that had happened. Laban's delight at his nephew's surprise appearance broke the latter's pent-up dam. Jacob's words flew out in a ceaseless torrent. His uncle was a rapt listener.

That night when he laid down his head to sleep, Jacob's mind returned to the night when *Adonai* met with him. From there in his lonesome wandering he had been led to this destination in the most amazing way. The cloud of despair that had hung over his speedy departure from home was replaced by a wondrous peace. Once enslaved by his thirst for intimacy, love, and recognition, a freedom he had never felt before engulfed Jacob. The trajectory of his life caused by his misdeeds had led him to traverse backwards the trail his mother Rebekah herself had taken to meet her husband-to-be, his *abba* Isaac. Life's irony was not lost on Jacob as he pondered his sojourn of banishment from his father's house only to end up wholeheartedly welcomed in his mother's house. A well of gratitude erupted in his soul.

The next day, Jacob awoke to a bevy of womanly giggles outside. Yesterday's events were no dream. His head had pillowed not on hard rock but on soft animal hair this time. And his aching body had enjoyed the covering of fine linen instead of his coarse coat. In that repose, Jacob opened his eyes. Looking around the tent, the sense of *Adonai's* presence startled him. Here he was in Haran. Land of his mother's family. Outside he could pick out the only voice that he wanted to hear. Rachel's. She was stunningly gorgeous with her raven black hair and ravishing figure. He had met Leah, Rachel's older sister with those captivating almond-shaped eyes. His tender heart went out to her affection for him. But it was Rachel who had Jacob entranced. Their first brief encounter at the well had been instantaneous attraction. Love at first sight. Jacob could not wait to get to know his cousin better.

In the month that followed, Jacob and Rachel stole every moment they could to be together. Alone. In that busy household and with a very observant father, privacy was a treasured commodity. Laban was obviously an astute and shrewd man. Jacob recalled his mother's telling of how it was her brother Laban who, quickly noticing the jewelry gifted her by Eliezer (*abba* Abraham's faithful servant sent to find a wife for his son, Isaac), was the one who had rushed out to meet the servant with the rich gifts. And it was Laban who quietly urged their father, Bethuel, with a knowing look to willingly verbalize their approval of a betrothal between Rebekah and cousin Isaac. Now Laban stood once more in the position of authority over a marital future, this time of Jacob and his own younger daughter.

Jacob hastened to make himself useful in his new home. No task asked of him was too menial or difficult. Laban soon found his nephew to be not only a strong man but also an affable one with an uncanny way with both people and animals. He had a surprisingly sharp mind and was a quick study in business transactions.

One day Laban made a proposition.

"Jacob, you're my beloved sister's son. Sent by your parents themselves into our family's care. Now here you are, a full month on and you have not taken our hospitality for granted. Instead you have freely made yourself very useful. Why should you not be paid just because you're my nephew? That is not right. Come, I am a fair man. Tell me tell me what would be a fair wage for your continued services."

This was the opportunity Jacob had been waiting for! Without hesitation, he answered Laban.

"Uncle, I am beholden to you for you have been nothing but gracious and welcoming of me, a stranger though related. It has been my pleasure to serve you. But since you ask, may I be so bold as to request my cousin Rachel's hand in marriage. In exchange, I will work for you. For seven years. If you would agree to my proposition."

Silence reigned for several long minutes as uncle and nephew contemplated the unordinary offer. How Jacob came up with that number both bewildered and delighted Laban. He was not about to refuse a good deal when he saw one. But not wanting to seem overly eager, he took his time to provide his response.

"Seven years, you say?" Laban asked.

"Yes, seven years, uncle. Seven years of my good labor for Rachel." Jacob repeated.

Jacob held his breath as he searched his uncle's face for a clue. Rachel had told him that her father loved nothing better than to bargain. So Jacob knew not to propose a transaction too simple as to make Laban think lowly of him, nor too onerous for his relationship with the woman he loved.

Rachel and Leah had been eavesdropping outside. The sisters held hands in collective suspense. Leah too had secretly fallen for the handsome Jacob. She had hoped that perhaps he would have considered the cultural tradition of the older daughter marrying first and would look her way. But it was only too obvious that Jacob had been smitten by her sister and she with him from their very first encounter. Leah loved Rachel too much to try and stand in her sister's way. They were best of sisters and best of friends. Rachel's well being and happiness had been Leah's responsibility ever since their beloved mother had passed to the other world a few years back.

After what seemed like an eternity, they heard their father speak again.

"It is with much consideration that I am giving you my answer, Jacob. Although it is not our tradition for the younger daughter to marry before her older sister, I have seen Rachel following you around like a faithful lamb. You have obviously caught her heart very early on. But there is the serious matter of our culture." Laban said.

This last statement hung precariously in mid-air. Laban looked intently at Jacob for any sign of wavering on the latter's part.

"Rachel and I have talked and thought much about this matter as well, Uncle." Jacob replied. "It is for this very reason that I am prepared to work for you for seven years. Not two or three, but seven," he reiterated, "with the great hope that by then Leah would have found herself a suitor deserving of her love."

Laban was pleased with his nephew's thoughtful response. "Well said, Jacob. You are a man of kind disposition and wise as well. Yes. Stay here with us. Seven years is a fair number. By that time too Rachel will know for sure if you are the right man for her." He smiled at his future son-in-law. "If she is still as much in love with you then as she is today, I will give you my blessing. To my mind it is far better that she marry her relative than some outsider."

With this, Laban removed his sandal and gave it to Jacob as a sign of their mutual agreement. It was a good marital match witnessed by both parties. Both men stood up and kissed each other on the cheek. The grin on Jacob's face was as wide as the river Euphrates. Laban knew he had secured the better deal but he was not about to let his nephew know.

Outside, the two sisters danced! Their relief and merriment, uncontainable.

It did Jacob's heart good knowing he had bargained rightfully for his bride. Jacob had come to his mother's home with specific instructions to find a wife for himself from among his maternal relatives. He had come with nothing save the clothes on his back, on the camel that carried him, and a loadful of emotional baggage. Now he had not only successfully found a wife but a vivacious beautiful young woman who made his heart turn with her every move. Truly *Adonai* was with him. The bride price would seem like a few days for he and Rachel were so much in love. But he didn't tell Laban that he had found a leather pouch among his belongings one day. Inside Rebekah had slipped a gold ring and one of her own wedding bracelets. Jacob smiled to himself when he weighed the two pieces of his mother's jewelry in his hands. His mother was ever thoughtful of her favorite son. Subtle to the core. On his wedding day he will place the ring and bracelet on Rachel's hands himself. But not yet. He sighed with contentment at the way things were turning out.

So Jacob worked seven willing years for Rachel. Laban was of fair means when Jacob first met him. But not wealthy. Not by any true measure. Jacob's father, Isaac, on the other hand, was wealthy. Immensely so. For not only had his *abba* Abraham left everything he owned to Isaac after he had breathed his last at age one hundred and seventy five, Isaac had been blessed by *Adonai* a hundredfold with his crops, flocks, herds and servants. Why, even the Philistines had envied Isaac and made futile attempts to clog up the latter's wells to no avail. Jacob knew true wealth. He also understood the land and reveled in hard work. While his twin Esau thrived on hunting, Jacob had been at his father's side. Watching, learning, and acquiring skills gained only through experience. Shepherding was Jacob's specialty. Nothing relaxed him more than being out in the open pastures with the sheep flock as they grazed. And nothing pleased him more now than when Rachel came along. Where once herding and watering her father's sheep were Rachel's responsibility, now her hours were happily spent sharing the work with her beloved Jacob. He was eager not only to please his future father-in-law but also to earn Rachel's trust.

Seventeen

LEAH

At first Leah was as delighted for her sister and even lived vicariously through the new couple's romantic spell for the first little while. After all, Leah had grown up giving in to the happiness of everyone else. Her parents loved their gentle oldest daughter. Leah was by nature kind and affectionate who always had a good word for others. When baby Rachel came along with her sparkling personality and big lustrous eyes relatives and friends began to comment on how Leah's eyes were smaller though tender in contrast. Leah merely shrugged her shoulders, laughed at the seemingly trivial comparisons and carried on. Together they grew up, the two sisters did, like most girl siblings. The older loving, caring, sometimes chiding, mostly gently leading. The younger adoring, playful, sometimes following like a lamb, other times stubbornly arguing like a petulant child. But ever since Jacob came into their lives, things had changed between the sisters.

Now as the days passed, Leah began to see less and less of her sister as Rachel made every excuse to be with Jacob.

Over the seven years from sunrise to sunset, Rachel was caught up with the giddiness of infatuation. Their father was caught up with the idea of having his sister's son working for him. For free!! Jacob was caught up with showing Laban how industrious and business savvy he could be. Leah soon found herself caught up in a tangle of suppressed resentment and pent-up emotions that was becoming increasingly difficult to hide.

"Would you believe it, dearest Rachel? Tomorrow is the day!" Jacob enthused.

Teasing her beloved, Rachel feigned surprise. "You mean you have been keeping count all these years, Jacob?"

"Of course! To the minute from the time that your father and I agreed upon the terms of my employment," he winked. "An hour worked is an hour closer to our wedding, my love."

Rachel could hardly believe her good fortune. That a routine walk to water her father's flock would one day lead her to her husband! A fine featured man, strong of heart and hands. Yet tenderness emanated from his soul whenever they were together. With her he spoke freely unafraid to share his dreams and desires. Even unabashedly confessed to her one day his penchant for cooking. She longed to hold him when in a trembling voice he disclosed his loneliness being far from his own family. Such an honorable man Jacob was, and the son of her father's very own relative. When Rachel sometimes innocently divulged parts of their conversations to her sister, her words gushed out in dizzying lyrics, unaware that the intimate revelations were creating in Leah a tumult of longing of her own.

Laban was an observant man. Nothing went unnoticed by him. Not Jacob's competence and savviness, nor his desire to keep his side of the agreement. Not Rachel's love-sickness, nor her naivete. And most especially not Leah's motherliness, nor her quiet disappointments. No, Laban was an observant father. And he was determined to observe the customs of his people and abide by his responsibilities as an honorable father. He would silence the behind-his-back whispers of relatives and neighbors once and for all with a scheme so deft it would be unforgettable.

Expectedly, Jacob came to speak with him exactly seven years to the day of their mutual agreement. Without a doubt his nephew had prospered in the safety and hospitality of Laban's household. Had enjoyed the adoration and love of his daughters. Most importantly, he had increased Laban's possessions and prosperity. Abundantly. Laban was pleased. Profusely so. He had been looking forward to this conversation.

"Shalom, uncle Laban. This day has come and not a minute too soon!" Jacob was thrilled beyond measure. He had bargained and labored for his bride. Now for the claim.

"Shalom, shalom, Jacob, my beloved sister's son. May your mother be blessed. Come, let us eat and enjoy a hearty meal to celebrate! Seven years ago you came to join our family. What a wonderful surprise that was. I was never more glad to offer my nephew refuge when you needed it. Rebekah, your dear mother, knew I would always welcome her kin. She did well to send you our way." Laban's circuitous reply brought both men back to that fateful day. It did not seem that long ago. But Jacob was impatient to get to the heart of the agreement.

"It is true and I am thankful to have been so warmly received by you, uncle Laban." Jacob replied. "You and my cousins have shown me what family is. Much as I sought refuge for a season, I also came in deference to my parents' wishes to find a wife from among their relatives. Except I did not expect to find her so fortuitously and speedily. Within your very own household. Rachel and I have been blessed indeed to have found each other. But, as agreed, I have won her hand not behind your back, uncle. But by mutual agreement and good, hard work." he reminded.

"That you have right, Jacob. I couldn't agree more. If I remember correctly, you won my Rachel's heart ever so swiftly. With that show of prowess at the well. Your solo removal of the hefty stone cover!" Laban chimed.

Jacob smiled at the memory of that fateful day. *"Adonai* be praised. He led me so directly to that watering well. And to Rachel. Whose very hand in marriage I now come to claim today. As we both had agreed upon."

"Ah, yes, the marriage. I have not forgotten, Jacob. But first, a toast. A toast before serious talk. Leah, come, bring out my finest wine. Jacob here has completed his obligation and is here to claim his prize." Laban called out to his eldest daughter.

But before Leah could respond to her father's demand, Rachel was already walking with two cups, a jar of Laban's favorite grape harvest wine and the widest grin on her face. Yet again, her younger sister had beaten her to the chase.

Laban was surprised to find Rachel and not Leah so quickly at his side.

"My beautiful Rachel, where is your sister? I called for her to bring me the drink." Laban asked.

"*Abba,* I knew you would want to celebrate this important day. So I was ready even before you called." Rachel smiled demurely at both men.

Jacob's heart was full, ready to burst with excitement at the sight of his betrothed standing before them, wine in hand. He marveled that she could so expertly pour the drink for them without a single drop of spillage. Her eagerness matched his and both their joy was obvious at this time.

'L'chaim, Jacob!' Laban held out his filled glass of the luscious red juice to his future son-in-law.

'L'chaim, uncle Laban!' Jacob responded, glass held high, and a delighted twinkle in his eyes as he looked at Rachel.

Standing in the kitchen, Leah felt never more alone watching the three favorite people celebrate without her.

After drinking their toast to life, Laban and Jacob settled into the serious talk of the wedding. Rachel sat by them drinking in every word of the arrangements. It was not their custom to have the bride-to-be involved in pre-nuptials but their mother was no longer with them. Laban instead summoned Leah to join them for she would be responsible for seeing to all the details of the auspicious day. The dates and times were set. Much preparations began in earnest thereafter. Rachel was giddy with excitement as she and her sister gave directions for the celebrations. It would be a busy seven full days of festivities with music, dancing, food and joyousness. Laban would spare no expense for the occasion. His household was a whirl of activities. Garments were sewn. Lamps polished. Healthy lambs selected. Elaborate food prepared. Wines chosen. The blasting *shofar* shined sparkling bright.

Jacob's parents were not with them for Isaac to present the bride's father with the dowry. But as earlier agreed upon, Jacob had himself paid for the dowry with his seven years of free labor. Jacob recalled his mother's wise words, "He who finds a wife finds a great good; he has won the favor of *Adonai.*" In Rachel, Jacob had found his great good and though the seven years of betrothal was unusual it was well worth every minute of the wait. In those seven years Jacob and Rachel had been able to get very well acquainted. Better than any other couple Rachel had ever known. Now all that was left was the wedding day.

Eighteen

LEAH & RACHEL

For seven nights festive celebations had been held in honor of the bride and groom. Rachel was delirious with all the merry-making. Overjoyed at the final arrival of this night, Jacob felt light headed with all the frenzy, the *mikvah* dancing after the sanctification bath, and the drinking. So caught up was the bridal couple by the pending consummation of their marriage that they were unaware of a sudden change in Leah's disposition. Nor of the determined look on Laban's face.

By the time Jacob carried his veiled bride to their bridal chamber, he promptly plonked into bed, and was gone. His mother's jewelry remained cleverly hidden in the pocket of his wedding tunic. His bride slept with him by his side, still dressed in her wedding clothes. The exhilaration and exhaustion of the last seven days had completely washed him out. The next day Jacob stirred awake only when he heard what seemed like sobbing. Puzzled by the sound, he turned to lift the veil that covered his bride's face. There staring up at him, her face wet with tears of shame and fear, was Leah. In the marriage bed!!

Jumping up, Jacob cried out, "Leah! What are you doing here?!!"

Aggrieved by the situation that she had found herself in, Leah was too incoherent to make any sense. Jacob stumbled out of their marriage tent in confusion. He tore into his father-in-law's tent demanding an answer.

"Laban, what have you done? Why is Leah in my bed? Where is Rachel?" The torrid questions flew unabated.

But before Laban could answer his new son-in-law, Jacob had pushed his way past Laban looking for Rachel.

"She is not here, Jacob. She has been sent to stay a few days with a family friend." Laban's calmness seared into Jacob's back.

"What is the meaning of this, Laban? We had an agreement. Seven years of toil and sweat serving you. For Rachel. Not Leah. Rachel! I have more than honored my word. And my work. I have more than tripled your wealth. Why have you done this despicable thing to me in return?!" Jacob screamed.

"Do you not for a minute think I too am an honorable man, Jacob?" Laban quietly replied. "Do you think I will dishonor my reputation in the community? Do you think I will dishonor my eldest daughter by letting her younger sister wed before her?"

Before Jacob could say another word, Laban continued. "No, I am an honorable man, Jacob. And because I am honorable, I will also give you Rachel in exchange for another seven years of work for me. But first you must finish Leah's bridal week as her husband. Within the week you will have both of my daughters as wives. This is more than fair, don't you agree? "

Laban's question hung in the air as the two men stared at each other. A thousand furious thoughts raced through Jacob's mind but he knew that there was nothing he could do to undo Laban's trap. Cursing his own lack of perceptiveness, and deeply concerned for Rachel, Jacob reluctantly agreed to the old man's contrivance.

"One week. One week I will share my tent with Leah, and not a day more. Only because I have long ago pledged my love to Rachel. Only because she is more deserving of a real man who loves her enough not to desert her in her time of greatest embarrassment and grief. Only because I will honor her reputation as a virtuous woman. No more trickery on your part, Laban, and I will serve you for the next seven years. And, mark my words, I will be watching your every move."

Jacob's answer satisfied Laban. Immensely.

"Agreed, Jacob. And to show you my gratitude for your understanding of our customs, I will give to you as well, in addition to my two beloved daughters, Zilpah and Bilhah, as each of their respective personal maids." Laban never felt more beneficent in his entire life.

Jacob left his manipulative father-in-law in disgust.

Storming back to his tent, Jacob found Leah still dressed as his bride, cowering in a corner, her back turned to him. Like a blind mole-rat trapped, unable to find its way to its underground burrow. Pity overcame Jacob's fury at the sight of Leah's distress.

"Leah," he gently touched her back. "Leah, please, get up. Please, look at me."

At the sound of his tender voice, Leah slowly raised herself up but she could not bring herself to face her now husband. Placing his big hands on her shoulders he turned her to face him. With all the calmness he could muster he lifted the bridal veil kindly. Her downcast eyes pooled with tears. His right hand lightly lifted her sunken chin.

"Leah, I am not angry with you though all of my insides tell me I ought to be. I know you had no choice in what happened. It is your father who deceived us. Not you. I know you could never hurt Rachel that way. Please, will you please tell me where she is? I must go to her and assure her of my love, my faithfulness." Jacob pleaded.

Shamefaced by the detestable duplicity she'd been forced to comply with, Leah stuttered out a name Jacob's ears could not make out.

"Leah, please, I'm not going to hurt you. Just tell me where your sister is." Jacob repeated.

"Zarah. Rachel is at the home of our friend, Zarah, Jacob." Leah said. "Go quietly by the less traveled south road where you will not be seen. Zarah's father has sworn to protect Laban's connivance. But her mother will find a way to let you speak with Rachel. Hopefully the girls have not been sent elsewhere by this time, yet." Leah offered up the whereabouts of her sister.

"*Toda raba,* Leah, I will not forget this!" With those words, Jacob hurried out.

Despondently, Leah muttered, "Pretend that you're going to drown your sorrows at your friend Solomon's. Zarah's place is two stone-throw away, left of Solomon's tent. Quietly. You know my father has loyal friends and relatives who insist on traditional ancient ways."

Leah had no idea if Jacob heard her warning or if her words were eaten up by the burning noon day sun. Drained and dejected she sat on the edge of the bridal bed inwardly hating herself for her timidity. Her inability to stand up to their loathsome father with his repulsive underhandedness. Her sense of servitude to her beautiful spoiled sister. For once she admitted to herself that Rachel was a minx, spoiled by her beguiling features and her coquettishness. Spoiled by the adulation of the entire village who saw her only in comparison to her plain older sister. Spoiled by Leah's doting devotion. Her hidden jealousies ate away at her broken heart. The look of pity on Jacob's kind face made her only more miserable. She yearned for his love, not his pity. She laid herself down on the bed and wept at the cruelty life had dealt her.

In what seemed like a lifetime as he stole his way to find Rachel, Jacob prayed. He prayed that Rachel would still be at her friend's. He had to assure her that he had not slept with Leah. That his love of those seven long years remained pure in every way, saved for her and her alone. Finally arriving at Zarah's place, Jacob hid himself and watched. Seeing no one about, he crept to the side and waited with bated breath for any sign of movement inside. Soon voices could be heard. Female voices. Taking his chances, he whispered, "Zarah."

Instantly, the tent flap flew open and Rachel's face appeared. "Jacob! It's you! How did you find me?"

A hand pulled Jacob inside. Three astonished women stood staring at him. "Shhh. Not a word. My husband will be back any minute. Go to the marketplace. I will send the girls to old Moshe's, the potter. He has a shack behind where he makes his pottery. Moshe is a deaf but a trusted friend. You can speak there. But make it quick before customers come to the store."

Jacob was very thankful for the prompt instructions. Without a word he traced his steps to the designated potter's place. There he pretended to look at the pottery for sale. Before long Zarah and Rachel showed up. With a slight nod of her head, Zarah indicated that she would stand guard while Rachel and Jacob slipped into the back. Old Moshe had shuffled his way to the front when he saw Zarah.

"Jacob, O Jacob. How you must hate me! *Abba* Laban had me fooled saying that he had arranged for me to stay with Zarah's family until it was time for you and I to be wed. Once I was there, Zarah's father became a tyrant and barred me from going out. Zarah told me what her father had agreed to do for *abba*. How could Leah agree to *abba's* deplorable scheme?!! " Rachel wept as the words tumbled forth.

"Shhh … hhh, Rachel. Do not cry. And do not blame Leah. She had no part in your father's madness. I made Laban tell me the truth. He is not the man I thought he was." Jacob held his beloved to his heart as he consoled her.

"All has been made right again, Rachel. By this time next week, we will be man and wife. Laban gave me his word."

"You believe *abba* after all this? How can you trust his word any more, Jacob?" Rachel gasped.

"I agreed to work another seven years for him." Jacob confessed.

"O Jacob, seven more years of bondage? Why?" she asked, confused.

"It is all arranged, Rachel. We will be married this time next week so the next seven years will be different." he assured her.

"But what about Leah?" Rachel continued.

"As of yesterday Leah is legally my wife, Rachel. Laban refused to undo his wrong. But I have not consummated our relationship, Rachel. Leah will be my wife only in name. You are my one and only love. She will not share my bed. I will make that very clear."

"O Jacob, Leah knows of our love. She has never spoken against it. But she is now your first wife and I will be the younger wife. What will that look like for us? To share a home as sisters will most definitely be different from sharing a husband!!" Rachel looked askance at Jacob.

"Do not ask me questions now I have no answers for, Rachel. We will make it work somehow, I promise you. What is crucial is that no one can come between our love for each other. No one! Not Leah. Not even your father. Not now. Or ever!" Jacob assured Rachel.

Before Rachel could respond to that doubtful assurance, old Moshe returned prompting Rachel and Jacob to quickly step apart. Zarah came in after the potter.

"Rachel, we must get back before father returns otherwise mother will be in trouble. *Shalom ve lehitraot,*

Jacob. Go! Go! You will see Rachel again. Soon, I promise." With that Zarah grabbed her friend by the hand and hurried themselves home.

Jacob turned to see old Moshe give him a kind knowing nod and his toothless grin. Jacob's heart pounded in his chest. What would his parents say to him about marrying not one but two women? Sisters both!!

The look on Jacob's face when he returned told Leah that he'd met with Rachel. Suddenly she became sensitively aware of his close physical presence. They had been together before but never in such awkward privacy. Jacob too felt nervous.

"Leah, thank you for your understanding. I did not have time to tell you earlier but I have made arrangements with your father that Rachel and I will be recognized, rightfully, as husband and wife. I will continue to work for him for the next seven years for this right. However, he insists that tradition must be abided by. So, Rachel and I will first have to wait out the customary bridal week between you and I. I will not embarrass you by insisting on a divorce. This mess is no fault of yours. You will, by the law of our forefathers, remain as my first wife. But understandably in name only. I have promised Rachel this. I will provide for you as your husband. That is expected." Jacob had never before in his life made such a long speech to anyone, much less to a woman. One who was officially his wife! This situation was a true conundrum which in all reality he had no solution for.

"Thank you, Jacob, for not demanding a divorce. It is my father who should be ashamed of his sly. You are a good man. Rachel is blessed to have such true devotion. I do not intend to come between your love. But I will insist my father give Zilpah and I our own accommodation after the week is done." Leah replied. Her unexpected response amazed Jacob and for the first time he saw into the heart of a righteous woman. Admiration for Leah welled up in his grateful heart.

There was no fanfare this time. No week of rousing festivities. No boisterous drinking among the men or endless dancing among the women. All that had been done at the initial wedding. But this time, a week later, in full view of all present, Jacob produced his mother's jewelry. Their eyes met, his and Rachel's, in determined union as he tenderly slid the ring and bracelet onto Rachel's finger and wrist.

Strangely the new marriage arrangement was accepted by everyone. It was as if it was normal. As if to be expected. Jacob could not get his head around the peculiarity of it all. That night in the stillness of his heart Jacob wondered what had become of *Adonai's* "I will be with you" promise. Was the Holy One with him in this despondent chaos of his life?

With his status among the elders intact, Laban happily acquiesced to Leah's demand for separate living quarters for herself and her maid. Rachel and Jacob soon settled into their own home. Jacob continued to work for his father-in-law. Peace and harmony was soon restored to the surprise and relief of the sisters and Jacob.

However, the relationship between Leah and Rachel was no longer the same. Both sisters were acutely conscious of being married to the same man though Jacob kept his promise to remain faithful to Rachel. But marriage was not all that Rachel thought it would be. Jacob loved her. She knew that.

He also was more wary of Laban and determined to quietly amass stock of his own. Enough to gain his independence and return to his own home one day after his years of servitude was completed. Rachel now had lots of time on her hands when Jacob was at work. The courtship was over but her expectations of her husband's attention to her was not. In fact, her sense of insecurity only heightened. She desperately wanted to be with child. To secure her rights as the bearer of her husband's heir. But the months of infertility crept by to her dismay. Rachel's sulking and petulance began to wear on their relationship.

As time went by, Jacob began to appreciate Leah's quiet reserve. She went about life with much grace and dignity as the first wife. Any gossip about her was quelled by her good-heartedness and seeming lack of resentment. Always thankful for Jacob's provision and protection as he had promised, Leah diligently watched over the affairs of Jacob's growing business. Together with her maid, Zilpah, meals for his workers were prepared without complaint and served with smiles.

One day out in the fields, his friend Solomon made a remark that got Jacob thinking.

"You know, Jacob, Matthias is much like you. A good man. Strong, smart, productive. Though you're stronger and smarter. Don't tell him I say so." Solomon chuckled at his own joke.

"And?" Jacob asked. "I'm waiting…"

"Well, he is now a father of three sons. In four years! You know what I mean?" Solomon winked.

"It is not for want of trying, Sol." Jacob replied. "Rachel makes sure of that." he winked back.

"That's what I'm trying to tell you, my friend. Like you, Matthias has two wives. Eliana, the younger, could not bear a child. Not at first. But after Talia, his first wife, gave him two healthy boys, Eliana conceived. Call it superstition or old women's tales, but word has it that oftentimes fertility in one is prompted by that of another. Now no one in Matthias' household is sulking," Solomon continued.

"Sol, you wicked man. I promised Rachel my faithful love from even before we were man and wife." Jacob gave his best friend a friendly shove.

"Jacob, Jacob! I know you're a man of your word. But a man needs sons. Surely Rachel would share her husband's happiness when, not if, his seed bears fruit regardless of from whom. After all, Leah is family, and who knows what could happen once one seed bears fruit!" Solomon bantered.

"You think Rachel would be agreeable, Sol?" Jacob wondered aloud.

"Rachel knows it is not uncommon. She grew up here. Talk to her. You've got nothing to lose. Except perhaps a day or two of silent treatment. Your happiness is her happiness. Just give it a try." Solomon was a convincing friend.

That night after dinner, Jacob sheepishly broached the subject. "I promised you my faithful love, Rachel. That will never change. But you know a man needs sons," he bravely repeated Sol's line. "At least think about it? Please?" he added.

Rachel was not shocked. Just annoyed with herself that it had come to this. Her barrenness gnawed at her like a relentless locust. She wished their *imma* was alive to share her wisdom. Reluctantly she walked to her sister's.

Leah was taken aback. "Are you sure that you want to do this, Rachel?"

"No, I don't want to do this, Leah. Every fiber of my being yearns to give Jacob a child myself." Rachel's frustrated retort came like lightning. "Not that I have anything against you, Leah."

"Then don't, Rachel. Nobody can force you," her kind sister replied.

"That's exactly it, Leah. It is up to me now it seems. I wish Jacob hadn't brought up the matter. But he did. He has. I love him with all my heart. And even though he has never made a fuss I have seen how natural he is with children. How his face lights up chatting with little Shmuel and Elijah next door." Rachel sighed.

"There is no guarantee that I will be able to give Jacob a child." Leah said. "Who knows, the problem might not even be with us!" as she tried to cheer Rachel up with a naughty laugh.

Arm-in-arm the sisters walked to the springs in the hillside. It was their favorite childhood place whenever they wanted to be alone. Away from the watchful eyes and ears of others, there in the cool of the cascades they were always able to be themselves, sharing their hearts about everything and anything. Now the sting of barrenness and the enigma of marriage to the same man played on their minds as they waded into the refreshing waters. Then in a mysterious way Rachel's worry and anxiety at hand became less insurmountable.

"Jacob is right. Every man needs a son. I must not be selfish. Who knows what could happen after one is born to another? Perhaps Jacob's *Adonai* will favor me then." Rachel pondered long and hard, weighing pros and cons in the scale of her mind.

So it was that Leah became pregnant with Jacob's seed. Amazement, trepidation, excitement ran the gamut through the entire household. Solomon thumped Jacob on the shoulders, a manly thump of approval. Jacob could hardly contain his delight. His excitement became Rachel's excitement. And Leah? No word could properly describe the range of emotions that ran through the course of her pregnancy. She could hardly believe all the attention that was now being shown to her. Laban's eyes gleamed with satisfaction. He had done his daughters right by his schemes and now he would be rewarded with grandchildren.

So it was that a son indeed was born to Leah and Jacob. Her misery of being unloved had been seen by her husband's *Adonai* after all!

"Now my husband will love me," Leah whispered to herself as she cradled the child in her arms. So he was named *Reu'ven*.

A grand celebration was held. Jacob beamed with pride but not too much as to hurt his dearest Rachel. Her magnanimity surprised him. Made him love her even more. Assured of his continued love for her, Rachel shared the cooing over the boy. Her sister's son was their husband's son. Leah tried hard to share the child. She really did. But her desire for husband's love was met with hidden disappointment and not a little resentment. Then when she conceived again, nobody could be more surprised. Another boy was born! Her second son was given the name *Shimon* for his mother was convinced that the Lord had heard her silent cries of discouragement. The entire village congratulated Laban on his growing family. The grandfather reveled in their praises. The glint in Jacob's eyes made Rachel's heart glow. Her decision to be generous was paying off. Leah's busyness was lightened by the help of Zilpah and Bilhah for her sister had unstintingly offered the services of her own maid. So when yet another son was born to Leah and Jacob, baby *Levi* carried in him the hope of his mother. The hope that since she had borne her husband three sons Jacob would realize that he was inevitably joined to her. But that did not seem to do the trick. Jacob's love for Rachel was an unbreakable bond. How Leah envied her sister of what seemed to be such faithful love. When Leah held Jacob in her arms each time they made love she gave to him her entire self. But often in the height of their coming together he had instead called out the name of Rachel. Leah's pain deepened like a stinging thorn.

As Jacob thrived in the fruitfulness of his loins, so too his business flourished, much to his satisfaction. He counted the days when he could bring his wives and growing boys home to show Isaac and Rebekah. Jacob's parents were always in his heart. He held on assiduously to *Adonai's* indelible words spoken to him in his sleep that unforgettable night at Bethel. *"I will bring you back to this land; I won't leave you until I have done what I have promised you."*

Jacob's success became his father-in-law's pride. Laban secretly congratulated himself in his own manipulations.

Year after year his flocks and servants and possessions expanded. Praise and plaudits aplenty came his way each time business was transacted. Laban became the talk and envy of the neighboring villages. Then when Leah presented him with grandson number four, Laban felt like his heart could explode with deep contentment. For he had finally seen in his eldest daughter's eyes a new found joy as she surrendered her disillusionment with Jacob's love for her and resolved instead to praise the Lord for the gifts of her sons and enjoy her boisterous household. *Judah* lived up to his name. Each time his mother looked at him, her heart welled up with praise and thankfulness.

Leah's apparent fertility began to grate on Rachel. Not that her sister gloated over her. Not obviously anyway. Frustration with her own barrenness manifested itself in growing exasperation. Verging on despair she hurled her wretchedness at Jacob.

"Give me children, or I'll die!!" she'd vented one day.

Laden with weariness, Jacob bellowed back, "Am I God that I have the power to deny you children, Rachel? Is my love for you not enough, woman?!!"

A hush fell over Rachel's tent when her husband stormed out. She had never before heard such severe words from him. Somehow she found it hard to believe that Jacob did not perhaps have feelings for the wife who had borne him four strapping sons in succession. An insidious jealousy clawed its way into her darkening heart.

When Jacob returned that evening, Rachel presented him with a shocking order. "Sleep with Bilhah, my maid.

May she give birth to a son so that through her you and I too can build a family of our very own. Yours and mine, Jacob. Yours and mine alone."

Rachel's misery and anguish played out in those reckless words. A wife taunted by infertility was no match for Jacob's waning fortitude. He gave in to her pleas and slept with Bilhah. Lo, and behold, conceive Bilhah did! Vindicated, Rachel named the child, *Dan,* saying, "At long last! *Adonai* has validated me with a son to lay on my knees."

Jacob was relieved. Rachel's happiness was palpable as she bore little Dan in her arms everywhere she went. Jacob would never understand women. But understanding was overrated. His happy wife equated to a happy life for the couple. Jacob was not about to argue with that! Peace and joy reigned. For a time. Then Rachel came pouting again to him.

"Leah has four sons, Jacob. Sleep with Bilhah once more. A family is incomplete with just one child. Humor me, my love, this one last time. I promise I will not pester you any more hereafter."

Shaking his head, Jacob acquiesced. He could never win against her entreaties. And to his amazement and Rachel's utter pleasure *Naftali* was born of her maid.

"I have won! I have won!" Rachel cried out. "How I wrestled with my sister and I won!"

Rachel's daily strutting with her maid's two sons became an irritant to one and all. Behind her back, Reu'ven, Shimon, Levi, and Judah sniggered at their aunt's childishness. Soon, her younger sister's conceit began to jar Leah.

"I will show the impudent who has won!" Leah declared uncharacteristically. Turning to her maid, she said, "Zilpah, prepare yourself. Master Jacob will bed with you tonight. My sister must be taught a lesson in humility."

Poor Jacob. Torn between two wives he succumbed to both their demands. Who knew if their wishes would come true. He was not about to add more fuel to an already contentious household of warring wives and growing sons. And to everyone's astonishment, Zilpah did become pregnant.

"What good fortune indeed." Leah clapped her hands. "Baby *Gad* will always know of how he has returned good fortune to me."

As if to add to Leah's good fortune, a second child was born to Zilpah the following year. They named him *Asher,* the child of his mistress' happiness.

Jacob's graying hair stood in contrast to his father-in-law's dark curls. Eight sons to raise were beginning to wear on him. Laban, on the other hand, was not complaining about his growing brood of grandchildren. More robust boys to add to his already robust wealth. Laban rubbed his hands in glee whenever he watched the young ones playing in the fields.

Seething with unbridled competitiveness, Rachel would not be outdone. One day, during the wheat harvest, she came upon Leah's oldest, Reuben. Clutched in his hands were a bunch of mandrake plants. Curious, Rachel followed her nephew. She saw him enter his mother's tent with the fertility roots.

"What, I wonder, does my sister want with the plant? Is she not satisfied with six boys?" Rachel wondered, not with a little disquiet within her.

She poked her head into Leah's tent.

"Leah, I saw Reuben come in with a bunch of mandrakes. How did he come by them? They are so hard to find!" Rachel asked innocently.

"Rachel. Nice to see you too." Leah replied sarcastically. "Have you been spying on my boys, again?"

"Spying? What would make you think I was spying? Reuben was walking right past me in the fields. In a hurry, I might add. He wouldn't tell me when I stopped him where he got the mandrakes from. So, I followed him here."

"Reuben was just excited to show me the plant, Rachel. He was out in the fields as you say to help with the harvesting. You know how Jacob enjoys having his sons join him in his work. Apparently, one of the men accidentally dug up some mandrakes. Jacob told Reuben to bring it here to show me. It is uncommon, this plant is, as you yourself know."

"Leah, please, I beg you. I have not been able to bear any child of my own. Please give me the mandrake. Perhaps it will awaken the infertility in my barren body." Rachel pleaded.

Aghast with her sister's request, Leah retorted.

"Isn't it enough that you have the love of Jacob, my lawful husband? Isn't it enough that he adores you? Now you want to take my son's mandrakes too?" Leah scoffed back.

Leah's protectiveness over her son took Rachel by surprise.

"The plants do not belong to Reuben. They were found on Jacob's land by Jacob's servant. So, technically, they belong to Jacob. My real husband, I might remind you. He was always mine from the start and never yours until father cheated on us!" Rachel reminded her sister.

"So, what will you give me in return for the mandrakes, Rachel?" Leah adamantly stood her ground.

"Very well, if you insist on an exchange. A night in Jacob's bed then for the mandrakes that Reuben brought you." Rachel offered without a moment's hesitation.

That evening when Jacob was coming in from the harvest, Leah went out to meet him.

"Leah, what brings you out to the fields this time of the day?" Jacob queried with a smile for his good wife.

"Why, Jacob. I have a surprise for you. Tonight you get to sleep in my bed because I have hired you from my sister in exchange for the mandrakes you'd sent me with Reuben." Leah's answer stupefied Jacob!!

"Hired?" Who did the two sisters think he was? A ram to be bartered for?

Jacob was too exhausted for any arguments. "O Leah, Leah, let me wash up and just give me my food. I have no energy for you women's pettiness."

That night Jacob slept with Leah. Thus Leah was rewarded with *Issachar,* the son she had won fair and square from her demanding sister.

Rachel could not believe Leah's luck. Four years her sister had not been in bed with her husband. And the one night she did, another son was conceived. In despondency, Rachel retreated to her tent. She didn't care where Jacob slept any more. It was belittling to be scorned by *Adonai.* She refused to be the laughing stock of the village. Then to her utter shock, Leah bore two more children for Jacob. A son, *Zebulun,* and a daughter *Dinah!* Their names were a just honor and exoneration for Leah but a deeply painful reminder to Rachel of her own impetuousness.

That's where Jacob found her. Sulking. Brooding. Inconsolably miserable. Without a word he held her in his arms as Rachel sobbed, her shoulders heaving in his tender embrace.

"I'm no use to you, Jacob. Not even the mandrakes worked for me! My shame is beyond imagination. What good is a wife whose womb is bereft, producing nothing, not even a daughter! Father was right after all to give you Leah. See how she has been so favored by the gods, unfailingly bearing you sons like your ewes in each lambing season."

"Shhh … my love, shh … my dearest Rachel. Why the bitter tears, cherished one? Is my love for you not worth more than ten sons? Jacob asked. "Has anyone dared to ridicule you? Tell me now and I will put an end to it at once!" he added.

"No, far from it. Everyone has been kind, Jacob," Rachel sobbed. "Too kind with their words. But their knowing looks … I want not their pity nor their sympathy. Is it so wrong to want your own child, my husband? Tell me what I need to do. I will do anything," she added.

Jacob sighed. Recalling Bethel where he had built his make-shift altar to the Lord who had come to him with angels in his sleep, Jacob tried to comfort Rachel. *"Adonai* once promised me descendants, my love. Let us not despair. Remember how He led me to you? Let us ask Him once more. Perhaps He will yet hear our pleas."

Looking down at his wife he found her more beautiful than ever in her vulnerability. How he longed to relieve her anguish. Disrobing with deliberate tenderness, their love-making that night consoled husband and wife.

And *Adonai* heard their whispered prayers. When Rachel's monthly curse did not make its clockwork appearance, she attributed it at first to her obsessive anxieties for a child. But when she found herself getting bone weary for no good reason and her period still missing the second month, her heart began to palpitate. "Could it be?" she wondered to herself. Nursing the flicker of hope she decided to keep the signs to herself. Life had been too full of disappointments for far too long. Better to wait for confirmation than be aggrieved yet again.

So it was that when by the third month she found her body unable to bear the taste of her favorite sheep milk and her breasts swelling and tender that she knew it was safe. Elated, she placed Jacob's big hands on her belly one night and drank in his surprise as she nodded her head in affirmation.

"Praise be *Adonai!!* Rachel, the Faithful One has heard our cries and answered." Jacob's voice quavered as his hands moved gently over Rachel's belly in scarce disbelief.

Leah was ecstatic with Rachel's news. All the rivalry between the sisters vaporized by the sheer miracle of the conception. Laban was so happy for his younger daughter that he gifted her with another maid to tend to her. "Just to see that you do not tire yourself with housework in your delicate state, my beautiful *bat*. First time with child is a fragile time. I remember well when your *imma*, bless her soul, was heavy with Leah. There was nothing I wouldn't do for her." He smiled at the nostalgic memory. He was a doting father and grandfather at heart.

Solomon clinked Jacob's cup in a congratulatory toast when his friend quietly came to share the good news one afternoon. "What did I tell you, my friend?! It took a while but what matters is Rachel is now carrying your son. I have no doubt it will be another boy. Mark my words. Sol is never wrong!" Jacob laughed at his mate's confidence.

B'sha'a tova wishes greeted Rachel's beaming face everywhere she went. Her good friend Zarah came as soon as she heard. The two women hugged and twirled in dance. "Now I know that truly nothing is impossible, Rachel!" Zarah sang out in happiness for her childhood mate. "You must come to our house! Mother will cook for you the most divine nourishing foods you've ever tasted. My mouth waters at the mere thought of it!" she laughed, chiding herself.

For the next six months, Rachel found her moods changing with her body. In the most unexpected good way. Womanly tales of a growing irritation and impatience as babies grew in their mothers' wombs did not seem to happen to her. She couldn't believe that pregnancy could be so exhilarating. Or that envy no longer filled her heart. No scathing sarcasm escaped from her mouth these days. Blissful as the ancient Abigail who sat in front of her tent each morning smiling her toothless grin, Rachel's days were now filled with delirious thoughts of motherhood and with preparations for the upcoming birth.

Leah readily shared her experiences of each pregnancy, willingly answering any question about what to expect for the birthing. "*Ayla* is the best midwife anyone can hope for, I tell you, Rachel. Wise and strong like an oak tree, her hands will guide your baby out into this world with the gentlest of tugs. She saw to all my birthings save one. "Issachar. He was breeched. And impatient to be expelled! But I will not scare you with that story. Your little one will come naturally and at just the right time. You'll see, Rachel. *B'sha'a tova,*" Leah repeated to assure her sister.

So it was that little *Joseph* came into the world, loved and welcomed more than any of his brothers had ever been. "May *Adonai* look kindly on us, precious *Yosef,* and add another in His good time. A brother of your very own to grow up with." Rachel whispered as she cradled her son.

When Jacob held Joseph in his arms, surprising tears welled up as he looked into the face of his tiny son. Their long awaited love child. His and Rachel's. Never in his life did he imagine that this could happen to him. *Abba* Isaac was an only child. Jacob himself was one of twin boys and that was it for his parents. Now here lay the eleventh son from his very own loins. After he had left home lonely and remorseful *Adonai* had seen fit to speak with him. Could this be the promise of descendants 'numerous as the grains of dust on the earth'? From as long as he could remember, Jacob had yearned to know the God of his *abbas* for himself. He had sought and struggled to be blessed by sheer cunning wit. Yes, he had stolen his brother's birthright and the blessing of the firstborn. But that had split the family and broken the hearts of his parents. At the very core of his being he was the cause of the rift and he lived with the guilt and shame of it every day. Jacob felt undeserving of any blessing. Yet here he stood. Two wives, two concubines, twelve children, good health and ever-increasing wealth. The fullness of *Adonai's* grace and mercy threatened to overwhelm Jacob.

Confused by her husband's unusual display of emotion, Rachel looked at Jacob with alarm. "What is it, Jacob? I thought our son would bring you the greatest of joy but here you are, tears streaming down your beard as if you've been stricken with sudden sorrow," she queried.

"No, no, Rachel, far from it!" Jacob answered at once. "They are tears of joy. That I have been so blessed of *Adonai* is beyond words. I just wish my *abba* and *imma* were here to share our joy. Here in the very village of Rebekah's own home."

Relief washed over Rachel. Jacob was always a sentimental man. It did her heart good to present him with their son. After all these years. *Joseph* was their most precious child.

Nineteen

JACOB & LABAN

Not long after the birth of Joseph, Jacob felt the time was right. He went to his father-in-law and said, "Laban, I have served you faithfully as I said I would. Some twenty years have gone by without a word of complaint. I want to bring my wives and my children to show my *abba* and my *imma*. Your sister, Rebekah, needs to hold her grandchildren. Send me back with your blessings as I had come with hers. Let me return to my own place, to my own home."

"Jacob, my son, why the rush? At long last my Rachel has finally presented me with her very own child. Your son is barely walking yet. And now you want to leave? Let Rachel recover and enjoy her new found joy a little longer. No, stay a while longer. Pray indulge a proud grandfather for another season at least. I have only one granddaughter. The little prince and precious princess need to get to know their grandfather Laban before being spirited away!" Laban reasoned.

When no answer was forthcoming from Jacob, Laban quickly added, "Name your wages, Jacob. I will readily pay them. I know you have *Adonai's* favor. And I have no argument with you that my blessing has been on your account. Come, name your wages!"

"Laban, your livestock have increased under my watch." Jacob affirmed his father-in-law's observation. "I want nothing from you that has not been honestly earned by the sweat of my brow. Now since you insist, I wish to leave with a flock of my very own. So here is my proposal. I will pasture your flock with the care I've always given to everything I do. In your full sight, I will pick out every speckled, spotted or brown sheep, and every speckled or spotted goat. These and their offspring will be my wages. No more, no less. When the time comes for us to part, you will inspect my livestock. If you find any sheep that is not speckled or brown, or any goat that is not speckled among them, then I am not a man of my word." Jacob said.

Surprised by Jacob's unusual proposal, Laban agreed. "Agreed! I couldn't have thought of a better plan. You, my son, are a man of temerity and sure integrity."

Secretly, Laban considered Jacob's proposal to be foolish. Could he not see for himself that the non-speckled livestock easily outnumbered the speckled and spotted ones? That white sheep and black goats filled the landscape? But he was not going to argue. Let Jacob get what he bargained for. Again. Laban's livestock was already larger than almost any other in the region. And it was going to be even larger by the time Jacob was done with pasturing them.

Losing no time, that very day Laban went through his flock. The streaked or spotted goats, male and female, and each one with white on it, as well as all the brown sheep, he put under the care of his own sons. To ensure Jacob would not suspect his early connivance, Laban separated himself and his livestock three days' distance from Jacob. Outwitting others was second-nature to him. His son-in-law would just have to learn the ways of the world the hard way.

Meanwhile, Jacob tended to his father-in-law's flocks, as agreed upon. He carefully peeled off the bark from fresh cuttings of poplar, almond and plane tree branches to reveal their white streaks. Standing them upright in the watering troughs they became clearly visible to the animals when they came to drink. When in heat, the flocks would come to drink and mate in front of the streaked branches and then produce off-springs that were not of one pure color. It was a breeding technique that Jacob had learned talking with the old shepherd, Elihu. The wise Elihu had not spent his entire life watching over livestock without learning some hidden nuggets about animal genetics and hereditary factors. Elihu had seen how Jacob had responded to Laban's double-dealing with an uprightness rare to most men. The two shepherds had struck a father-son like bond over the years of sharing many hours in the open fields. Elihu had also taught Jacob to recognize the sturdier animals and how to lure them as well to mate with the hardier streaked and brown flock. Jacob thus ended up with the stronger livestock and Laban the weaker. In due season, Jacob acquired healthy flocks of sheep and goats in addition to camels, donkeys, male and female slaves separate from Laban. Jacob became richer than he could ever have imagined.

But Jacob's success resulted in great jealousies among Rachel's brothers. Behind his back, they murmured. Convincing themselves that Jacob had amassed his wealth at the expense of their father, they spread their lies to Laban every opportunity they could. Word of their fabrication soon got to Jacob. This and Laban's changing attitude toward his son-in-law's reputation and growing prosperity were warning flags Jacob could no longer ignore.

Then one shocking incident helped make up Jacob's mind. *Adonai* spoke to him. Not since Bethel had Jacob heard again from the Lord. But clear as his speckled sheep, Jacob heard the words now, *"It is time, Jacob. Return to the land of your fathers and your kinsmen. I will be with you."*

This was all the confirmation he needed. Jacob got Rachel and Leah to meet him outside where he was with his flock. Looking around to ensure that no one else was around, Jacob then spoke.

"Rachel, Leah, you have heard me tell you that one day I will bring you and our children to meet my family. The time has come."

The two women looked at one another. They were not surprised by Jacob's words. Only by his apparent resoluteness.

"It is obvious to everyone that your father no longer looks at me the way he once did. Your brothers have been whispering falsehood into his ears. Despite all my years of honest servitude Laban has cheated my wages more times than I wish to recall. And disparaged me in front of the other men with his snide remarks. I will no longer put up with his thankless behavior." Jacob said.

Everything that their husband was telling them was true. They had seen it with their own eyes, heard their father's unkind denigration of Jacob with their own ears. Rachel and Leah had no words to counter Jacob's remarks.

"But *Adonai* has protected me. Despite your father's countless attempts to swindle and cheat me, cheat us, his very own family, *Adonai* has prospered us. He was the one who affirmed what old Elihu had taught me about mating the animals. Why, he even sent an angel in a dream to affirm to me all that Laban was doing behind my back. So, as I had vowed to *Adonai* at the standing-stone altar at Bethel, I will do as *Adonai* bids. We will leave for my home as led." Jacob was adamant.

To his great relief, both his wives answered in one accord. "Marrying us off, we no longer have any inheritance from our father. In his eyes, we were foreigners long ago, sold like cattle. As well, all that he received from our dowry he has depleted. We are your family, we and our children together. Whatever *Adonai* has taken away from our father to give us has been ours. Just say the word and we will follow where you lead, Jacob."

"Praise be *Adonai!* We are in agreement then. Shearing week will be upon us. Till then, discreetly prepare yourselves and the children. When Laban is away with the sheep, we will leave at once. But not a word to anyone else about this!" Jacob warned Leah and Rachel.

So much to do in that short time. Maintaining their composure amidst the excitement, trepidation, and not a little anxiety required great effort on everyone's part. None of them had ever ventured beyond the great river, Euphrates. Thankfully they lived some distance from Laban and were able to start their packing without suspicion. The day before departure, Rachel slipped into her father's tent and stole one of his household idols. She told nobody, not even her husband. He would most certainly not understand and make her return it.

They left. Jacob and his wives and children and vast household. It was no mean feat to steal away. Shearing would keep Laban and his sons busy for an entire week. It was only on the third day that word reached Laban about the secret exodus.

"What do you mean no one is left?" Laban queried the servant who had brought the stunning news. "Left for where?" he asked.

"Master, my son Adnan saw Jacob heading out toward the Gilead hill country. He has taken your daughters and their maids and your grandchildren with him. Including all their servants and livestock." the man replied.

A furious Laban rounded up all his relatives and set chase. He was familiar with the territory but Jacob had had a good head start. Seven days of relentless pursuit before catching sight of the escaping retinue. His own family. Laban knew the day would come for Jacob had made no secret of it. But Laban never reckoned to be so secretively abandoned. The very thought of it hurt his pride. He would make sure that Jacob paid for his indiscretion. But that night, Laban had a dream. God spoke a warning. *"Whatever you do, good or bad, to Jacob, be careful. My eyes are on all of you."* Cold sweat shook Laban awake. He was determined to tread cautiously.

Jacob was greatly disappointed that his father-in-law had caught up with them faster than anticipated. But he was resolute not to be swayed either way. Not by Laban, nor by any of his own family should they suddenly decide to return with Laban.

"Jacob, my son, why have you left without a word? Is this the way to repay the father of your wives who has been nothing but kind to you?" Laban asked.

"Laban, it was never my intention to deceive you. But you are a forceful man. There was no other way to leave. I know you would never have readily agreed to let us go." Jacob replied.

"You discredit me, my son. I would have given you a proper send-off, held a farewell celebration and blessed your return to your family home. I would have sent gifts with you for my beloved sister, your *imma* Rebekah." Laban countered. "Instead you have concealed your plans, leaving me not even the opportunity to kiss my daughters and my grandchildren goodbye!"

"Forgive me, Laban, but it is not once that you have not kept your word. Twenty years I have faithfully labored for you. Twenty! Seven for each of my wives. And another six years for your flocks. In those twenty years you have short-changed me of my rightful wages ten times. Not once, or twice, but ten! Can you fault me for no longer trusting you?" Jacob retorted not with a little impatience.

Ignoring Jacob's accusations, Laban lashed back. "But why have you taken my household gods with you? Taking your family is your right, I give you that. But you have no right to steal my gods!"

"Nobody stole anything from you, Laban. You are imagining things. I have no need of your household gods. They mean nothing to me. Do nothing for me. Go ahead and search for yourself. If anyone here is found with anything that rightly belongs to you, that person will not live." Jacob snapped back.

"You bet that if I find my property among yours, Jacob, that person will have much to answer to. I would have you trashed but for a dream from God last night warning me about you." Laban confessed reluctantly.

So Laban and his relatives began the search. From tent to tent they went. First Leah's, then Zilpah's. Nothing turned up. Then to Bilhah's. Still they came up empty handed. Lastly, Laban walked into Rachel's tent.

"Peace be with you, my dear father Laban," Rachel greeted him. "Forgive me for not standing up to greet you as I should. I mean no disrespect. But my monthly woman cramps leave me drained. Please search all you want while I remain seated."

At those words from his younger daughter, Laban made a quick comb of her tent. No idol of his was among her things. What a let-down. He was hopeful to use it as leverage to get his family back.

"What did I tell you, Laban? I have committed no crime. Done you no wrong. Yet you have the gall to come accusing me and my family of theft! Everyone here is witness to your shameless accusations and my innocence. What do you have to say for yourself now? *Adonai,* the great good God of my *abbas* Abraham and Isaac has faithfully watched over me. The Almighty One has seen all my toil and sweat, and observed your dishonest ways and has kept me safe. But for Him you would have left me destitute. He is the one who has prospered me." Jacob spewed out his years of frustration with his ruthless father-in-law.

Caught without defense, Laban demurred with this offering. "Let us part amicably, Jacob. After all, your wives are my daughters, your children are my grandchildren, your flocks originally mine."

"H-ow …" Jacob was stopped before he could go any further.

"Let me finish, Jacob. Like I said, I wish that we part in peace. Mine as they all are, pardon me, were, they are also rightfully yours. As you said, you have earned your keep. So, I propose a truce. Let us covenant here before everyone as witnesses. We will set up a stone pile between us. Mine will be called Mizpah, Witness Monument." Laban offered again. "May God keep watch between you and me, your family and my family. If you mistreat my daughters, or marry other wives, God will be the witness between us."

With this, Jacob agreed. He summoned his family to gather stones and made a heap. Named it 'Galeed'.

Needing to have the last word, as always, Laban added, "This stone monument will bear witness. I will not cross this line to harm you. And you will not cross it to harm me. May the God of Abraham and the God of Nahor, the God of your children's ancestors, judge between us."

In agreement, Jacob took the oath of honor to his father Isaac. He offered a sacrifice there and worshiped and held a feast of remembrance of their covenant. Everyone ate and slept that night on the mountain. The next morning, Laban arose early. Trying hard to check the unfamiliar tears coursing down his cheeks, he kissed his daughters and grandchildren and blessed them. Not trusting his own emotions, he swiftly swung his leg over his camel, leaned back on its saddle, and headed home. Leaving his family with Jacob, Laban gritted with resolve not to turn for a look. A bitter-sweet parting.

Rachel breathed a huge sigh of relief. The camel saddle with her father's idols hidden inside was the most uncomfortable seat she had ever had to sit on!

Leah breathed a sigh of relief. For the first time in her life, her father was no longer around telling her what to do, where to go, directing her every step, controlling her every movement. For the first time in her life she was seeing the world outside Paddan Aram. Her thoughts turned to imagining what Jacob's parents, Isaac and Rebekah, would be like. How would they react to their son's arrival home with his two wives and large family?

Jacob breathed a sigh of relief. Calm had replaced the stormy contention of the past twenty-four hours. He had almost lost the mind-game again with Laban but for his determined resolve to stand up to the man. As he journeyed forth, he contemplated the trajectory of his life. Had anyone told him when he ran from the wrath of Esau leaving the protection of home that he would be returning to his parents with wives, servants, eleven strapping sons, a daughter, and a handsome retinue of livestock and herds he would have scoffed at that craziness. Yet here he sat high on his camel leading his entourage. From the family of his uncle Nahor to go back to his own family, the family of his *abba Yit'zhak*. For once in a long long while Jacob felt like a free man. Freed from the penalty of his past deceptions. Freed from the weight of twenty years serving a shrewd, demanding and greedy uncle/father-in-law. No bitterness rankled his heart. No sourness marred their parting of ways. For that Jacob was most grateful. *Adonai* had safeguarded their departure. At this thought he lifted his eyes to the horizon. To his utter astonishment he saw a host of riders approaching. Instinctively something spoke to his spirit. *Adonai's* angels!! At once the vision of the angels ascending and descending the heavenly ladder twenty years ago resurfaced. He could not tell you how but he knew.

Leah and Rachel saw their husband raise his right hand signaling a stop. *"Machanayim!"* they heard him breathe out. "This is *Adonai's* very great camp. His celestial hosts have come to meet us." Jacob's joy could not be contained. The Almighty had sent his angels to escort them. His family was puzzled. They could not see what he seemed to be seeing. But his delight was palpable. They stopped as directed. And savored the rest from their journeying. Jacob alone savored the sweet fellowship of *Adonai's* very presence.

Twenty years ago a despondent lonely Jacob had been in exile. Till a holy encounter at Bethel encouraged spirit, mind and body to venture forth in faith. Now, twenty years later, a hope-filled *Adonai*-led Jacob was returning home.

The holy encounter at Mahanaim emboldened a confidence of no little means.

But for an all too brief spell.

Twenty

JACOB & ESAU

For soon the image of his embittered vindictive brother uttering murderous words as Jacob rode off twenty years earlier returned in full force to haunt him. Soon the familiar landscape reminded him all too clearly that he would be stepping into unpredictable territory around the bend. Who knew if time had indeed healed hurts and broken dreams. Especially if those dreams had been ruthlessly dispelled by one's very one flesh and blood. One's unexpectedly cunning twin at that. Perhaps the rift between brothers was unmendable. Perhaps blood-curdling enmity was their fate. Fear and doubt began to assail Jacob's once exhilarated composure. Once again uncertainty clutched his heart. And cowardly scheming began. In earnest.

Calling his two most trusted servants, Jacob gave his instructions. "Beyond is Seir where my brother, Esau, lives. You are to go to him and say, "Your servant, Jacob, who is returning from his lengthy stay with his uncle Laban is very pleased to be passing through his lord, Esau's land and greatly hopes to find favor with his lord. Your servant, Jacob, has cattle and donkeys, sheep and goats, and servants, both male and female."

Abishai and Ehud left with their master's message. But they returned only with alarming news. "Your brother Esau is coming to meet you himself. He rides with four hundred of his men."

That was the kind of news that Jacob had dreaded. Great distress drained his face. Plunging into defensive mode, Jacob divided his convoy into two groups. Should Esau attack, at least one group may escape. Too terrified to think straight, Jacob's panic-stricken mind went into overload. His sons and wives could not reconcile this fear-filled frenzied man with the peace-filled undaunted one a mere ten hours earlier. Then they saw him abruptly disappear into his tent with strict instructions not to be disturbed.

In the privacy of his enclosure, Jacob prayed. "O God of my *abbas* Abram and *Yitz'chak,* remember that in fear I had crossed this Jordan with nothing but my staff. I am unworthy of all the kindness and faithfulness you have shown your servant. You directed me to return home to my own relatives with the promise to prosper me. I have obeyed you. But now my life and that of my wives and children are in your hands. Save us, I pray in this time of terror from the violence of my brother. You have said that you will surely prosper and make my descendants like the countless sand of the sea. That will surely not come to pass now if you do not come to our rescue."

That night, Jacob felt it was incumbent to send a gift to his brother. It had to be generous enough to show his sincere contrition and to appease. With careful selection, he picked an extravagant tribute numbering five hundred and eighty of his best animals, male and female: goats, ewes, rams, camels, cows, bulls, and donkeys. Separating them into specific herds, he instructed his servants to go ahead, keeping some space between the herds. And if Esau were to query the largesse, tell him, "Your servant Jacob is coming behind us. He is pleased to send his lord Esau these personal gifts to you."

Jacob gave the same instruction to each of the servants leading each herd. With the repeated assurance, "Your servant Jacob is coming behind us."

With a prayer and a hope, the servants and herds were sent ahead to placate Esau. That night, he escorted Rachel and Leah, Zilpah and Bilhah, and their eleven sons and daughter, Dinah, across the Jabbok ford, followed by all his possessions.

Finally, Jacob alone was left. With his desperate thoughts and fears, each imagination of 'what if' scenarios escalated with the ticking seconds. The encampment of angels at Mahanaim was all but forgotten as his mind turned captive to his phobia. Did the God of angels himself hear his feeble prayer?

Jacob wondered if twenty years had changed his twin. Mellowed that quick temper of Esau's? Just as he himself was no longer the same man, Jacob hoped that Esau no longer held him in hatred and contempt. Perhaps even have forgiven him? But why then would Esau be accompanied by four hundred men? Even after having been told by Jacob's servants that Jacob was coming in peace. With only women and children; no intimidating contingent. Surely Esau's posse could only mean one thing—avengement!

Back and forth Jacob's mind swung, between hope and hopelessness, fear and faith. In a calculated risk, he had sent his family ahead with an earnest plea to *Adonai* for their safety. The battle with his brother was his to fight, not theirs to witness. Now he had to fortify himself for the confrontation. For a moment he remembered what *Adonai* had said. Had promised. Courage was called for now, not feebleness. *Adonai* had come to him in his most vulnerable of moments. Not once, but twice. The first time, two decades ago. The second time, a mere twenty four hours ago. It was to him, Jacob, son of Isaac, that the divine promises had been made. Jacob told himself to hold on to these personal divine encounters. His life depended on it.

So Jacob was left. Alone. Contending. Agitating with nervous energy. Foreboding the worst when a sudden movement shook him out of his petrified brooding.

"Who's there?" Jacob called out, fighting to still the quiver in his voice. His eyes darted across the bog in the darkness. "Show yourself instead of hiding like a coward!" He challenged the cavernous void.

By the light of the shadowy moon, the form of a man appeared. Jacob could not make out the man's face. Only the thuds of footfall approaching, closing in, matching the ominous thumpings in Jacob's heart. Could his brother have come so swiftly in the stealth of night?

Not waiting to find out, Jacob lunged at the man with the full force of his pent-up terrors. The man fought back with equal might. By the flowing Jabbok river the two men wrestled, the silence of darkness pierced by the heaving grunts of brute force. Jacob was not to be mollified. He had not come this far in life to be killed by a furtive stranger. Not when he was half-way home. Not when he had toiled under conniving Laban and was finally rid of his father-in-law. Not when the lives of his wives and children depended on his survival. Not when he had yet to face his estranged brother. Not when he had once personally met with the one called *Yahweh* and been promised a lasting legacy. For the life of him, Jacob would not be overwhelmed. Would not be yielded. Defeat was not an option.

Even when the first light of day began to break over the intense wrestling, unrelenting Jacob clasped his spent arms around the man's swarthy neck with his waning strength and clung on. When the man saw Jacob's ferocious determination to live, he smiled to himself. It was time. Jacob had shown his mettle. Met his own nemesis. Tasted his own fears and weaknesses. Not succumbed solely to his desire to return home but held on tenaciously to the covenant of *Adonai*. It was time.

Locking both his arms around Jacob's sweating torso with his full weight the stranger heaved Jacob to the ground unlocking himself from the latter's vise-like hold. Jacob's scream riddled the creeping morning. Hip wrenched out of joint. Yet his thick right hand grabbed onto the man's ankle.

"Let me go, it's daybreak!" the man commanded.

Writhing in pain, Jacob yelled, "I will not let go. Not till you tell me who ... who you are."

"Not till you bless me." He added boldly.

Ignoring Jacob's question, the man asked, *"What is your name?"*

"Jacob," he answered.

"No. Not. Any. Longer." The man's words panted out in staccato. *"From now on, you are no longer Jacob. You. Are. Israel. God Wrestler. Prince."*

Shocked by the mysterious words, Jacob could only think to ask one question. The same question. "What is your name?"

"No need to know. Suffice that you have shown your true strength. You have contended with Adonai. The Almighty himself now blesses you. You will no longer fear your brother. Your children will call you blessed. You have fought and faced your own enemy. Go and claim your abba's blessing" With that, the man disappeared just as he had ghostly appeared.

Sapped of all strength, Jacob lay on the creek bank panting, drawing long slow breaths in an effort to slow down the drumming in his heart. For what seemed like an eternity, he laid there. Alone, yet not alone. He felt it. Knew it. Did not quite understand it. The words of his mysterious contender ringing in his ears, dancing in rhythmic circles in his head.

'Israel' the man had named him. *'Israel—Wrestler'.* Not merely any wrestler, but God-wrestler. Slumped in breathless wonder, he whispered, *"P'ni-El. I have seen the face of God and lived."* Wrapping his mud-caked arms around himself, he wept.

Then as the sun inched its glorious way into the morn, he gingerly lifted up his spent body. A new day had begun. Jacob/Israel limped forward. Bent. Broken. Blessed.

Twenty years of separation from his twin, Jacob thought he had dealt with the regret. The pain. The shame. But with Esau now closing in nearer and nearer, hope and joy, fear and dread once again threatened to surface in a combobulated mess. Which mess he'd wrestled the night through and emerged, a new man. Israel will face his estranged twin. His nemesis. Peace pervaded his soul.

Looking up, he saw Esau in the distance accompanied by four hundred men. He had organized his family for their first encounter with his brother. Bilhah and sons, Zilpah and sons, Leah and sons and daughter, Dinah, Rachel and little Joseph. In that order. Could anyone hear his pounding heart, see his leaden feet as he moved step by step forward, eyes fixed on the man ahead of him? When he was within three camel strides of his brother, Israel eased the animal to the ground, carefully lifted his frame from the saddle, and humbly prostrated himself. Winching ever so slightly from his rawly disjointed hip, he touched his head to the ground seven times before Esau.

Moved by the sight, Esau dismounted from his camel, ran and grasped his twin by the elbow. The touch sent a tremor through Israel's shaking hands like a lightning shock. Eyes riveted to the ground, he slowly stood up.

"*Ya'acov,* brother, look at me!" Esau shook his brother. "Look at me!"

Hearing his familiar name spoken, Jacob raised his eyes to meet those of *Esav.* Tears glistened, then rolled unbidden. They embraced. Tightly. Their tumultuous past lost in the river of reconciliation. In silence they clung together. For seconds. An eternity. It was as if both men finally realized all that they had lost in the years of separation. They were brothers after all. Of the same mother. One father. Twins. How did they ever allow sibling rivalry to shackle their precious relationship? Why??!! The senselessness of it all. Family. Life was nothing without family. In that strong speechless embrace, forgiveness flowed from heart to heart.

In bewildered wonder, the others watched. Esau's four hundred men. Jacob's women and children. No one spoke. Each person watched, the emotional reunion etched in their communal memory. Forever.

Pulling himself apart, Esau spoke first. *"Ya'acov,* it's been too long. Where have you been? And where, may I ask, are you heading to? And who ... who are all these people with you, my dear brother?" Esau queried, pointing to all the people behind Jacob, the questions rolled.

"I am going back, *Esav.* Home ... to *abba* and *imma.* And these, these are *Adonai's* gracious blessings to me. My children need to meet their grandparents."

"All of them? Esau asked. "Yours, all?" He repeated, astonishment clearly evident in his voice.

"Yes, yes, each and everyone is mine." Jacob reiterated, somewhat proudly.

Then, with a sheepish grin, Jacob introduced his family. Esau watched in amazement as each one was introduced to him. From Leah to Rachel, Bilhah to Zilpah, Reuben to Joseph, each woman and son bowed, honoring their new-found relative. Looking from man to man, the family found it hard to believe that the men before them were twins.

Although the years had etched lines on their faces, Esau was still brown, brawn and hairy and Jacob stood an inch shorter, his skin two shades lighter, his shepherd's hands gentler. Only the brothers' broad-faced smiles gave them away.

"And what is the meaning of the large herd you sent ahead, Jacob? Not that I would not welcome my long-lost brother without gifts." Esau asked.

"They are but a small gesture of appreciation on my part, brother. I very much would like you to accept them, *Esav.* Please do me that favor," Jacob urged.

"But I myself have more than plenty. Keep what you have for your large family instead." Esau declared.

"No, please, *Esav,*" Jacob prevailed. "To see you and be welcomed is more than I could ever hope for. It is like seeing *Adonai* face-to-face. The Mighty One has been merciful and gracious. I went away with nothing. He is sending me home with this abundance to share. Please. I insist. For my sake."

"Alright, then, if you insist, I accept your gifts with gratitude. But let me at least accompany you home. I want to see the look on *abba* and *imma's* faces." Esau proffered.

"Your favor is all my heart needs. We will only slow you down." Jacob replied. He hesitated to add that he wanted his home-coming to be his alone.

Disappointed, Esau said, "Take some of my men with you then. The journey ahead is long and can be dangerous. They will be able to protect your women and children."

But Jacob gently answered, "*Esav,* you are too kind. *Adonai* will watch over us. There is no need to trouble your men. Let them return to their own families with you."

No one knew of his new name. There had not been time to share his sacred encounter. He kept it to himself. Needed to get a grasp of what 'Israel' really meant. Needed to, for now at least.

Esau saw that Jacob was adamant. His brother had changed. No longer the meek, conniving twin. Esau admired the quiet strength the man had acquired. Jacob stood amazed. Amazed at his brother's reticence, his gentle kindness diametrically different from the man whose heart had burned with murder toward him. As they kissed farewell, first on one cheek, and then on the other, it seemed like heaven and earth stood still to watch the reconciliation.

Hearts restored and a lifetime of wrongs, grudges and hatred behind them, the brothers parted. Peacefully. Esau's four hundred men followed their master back to Seir. Jacob and his family headed slowly for Succoth.

Joseph and his siblings silently watched the parting of the brothers.

Shalom.

"Thus Jacob came home to his father Isaac
in Mamre, near Kiriath Arba (that is, Hebron),
where Abraham and Isaac had stayed. Isaac lived a hundred
and eighty years. Then he breathed his last and died and was
gathered to his people, old and full of years. And his sons
Esau and Jacob buried him." (Genesis 35:27-29)

ACKNOWLEDGEMENTS

Reading and writing—two wonderful adventures that have brought me joy from as far as I can remember. To the Creator God who formed me and knew me before I knew myself, and who put those desires in my spirit, I give first acknowledgement of thanks and deepest gratitude. I pray that the stories you lay in my heart will point readers to you.

My good man, Chris, whose faith in me surpassed mine and whose years of patient urging to take that step of faith to publish, thank you for enduring my wrestling. You are the husband I needed and still do. Thank you also for being the best father to Ben and Joyce. You are their strong oak tree. From you they learned to encourage their mother in her own endeavors to discover herself. Ben and Steph, despite the physical distance that separates us, we know that your love for us is strong and always there. May you remember that while we are always here for you, God is even more dependable. Joyce and Wes, thank you for your willingness to share life with us in so many ways, big and small. Your creativity, Joyce, is a gift from God and I am blessed to have you as a daughter. Thank you for taking time amidst your busy life to design the book cover.

My thanks to Perry and Catherine Soh, long time friends, for your excitement and encouragement towards my writing efforts AND for connecting us with Angela Wagler. Angie, your enthusiasm to work with me to birth this first baby of mine has been a delight. I could not have wished for a better midwife. Your keen eye for details, editing skills, and professionalism led this long journey of mine into an adventure at the end. I am very thankful that our paths have crossed!

Dear Ruby Knudtson, friend and kindred spirit, who took it upon herself to not let me be until this book came to be, I am very grateful. You were my first reader and editor, helping me with your skills, comments and tireless cheering on. The good Lord alone knew when we first met on that trip to the Holy Lands where that encounter would take us. So, thank you, Ruby, for believing in me even when I did not always believe in myself. Carolyn Matiisen who readily agreed to read and edit, making sure my grammar and punctuations were proper, you are much appreciated. Rick Love, Pastor, Professor, Mentor, Friend. Your plate is overflowing with too many newcomers to help and ESL classes to run yet you took the time and trouble to read my manuscript and encourage my maiden writing effort. You are grace personified.

Christian author, Mark Buchanan, whose books speak into the hearts of countless readers, your gracious endorsement of a newbie author is more than I dared hope for. You have no idea how much your own writing has helped me. Merci beaucoup. Fern Buszowski, whose life and faith has become a beacon of hope for many in tumultuous days, I am grateful for your help and support. Peggy Epp who put me in touch with author Arlana Crane; Anne van de Vliert who connected me with author Leanne Paetkau, you all helped steer me toward the next step in the process. I am grateful. Arlana and Leanne, thank you for willingly sharing with a stranger your own publishing experiences. Your kindness reminds me of the family of Christ.

This book was undergirded by the prayers of a group of special people. I am blessed to have my sister, June Chia, and niece, Ruriko Apperson, whose faith is as deep and wide as the oceans that separate us yet you are ever ready to pray. Dear friends, Victor and Sophia Lun, Terry Muhn, Jill Ireland, Dennis and Ruby Knudtson, Anne and Henry van de Vliert, Shirley and Jiju Thomas, Queenie Hui, Chanhee Park, Meena Paul, Dee Harmer and Shirley Ryning who bless me with your faithful sacred friendship and precious prayers, Thank you, Thank you, Thank you!

37682774R00099